Ink & Ivy

<u>Books by Angela Grey</u>
Spirit Pass: A Jessica Stone Novella #1
Missing and Murdered Indigenous Women & Girls: A Jessica
Stone Novella #2
The Lasting Echo of Lost Souls: A Jessica Stone Novella #3
Resilience Throughout Recovery
Beyond Quirky
Run Fast, Run Far
Sifting Through a Storied Past
Coteau des Prairies Runaway
Prologue to an Epitaph
A Childhood Lost to the Wind
Secret Whispers
Déjà vu
Of Laughter & Heartbreak
Beating Drum of a Broken Heart
Nostalgic Tendencies, Idyllic Endeavors & Current
Inclinations
Between Shadows and Lies
Bedridden & Gutted to Mindful
Bdote
Dreamcatcher
The Cartography of First Love
Whimsy and Bliss

<u>Also by Angela Grey & Paige Peterson</u>
Lake of Secrets
Dancing Without Music
Echoes of the Past
Echoes at Midnight
Madness and Mayhem
Long Since Buried
Since You've Been Gone
Some Species of Outsider-ness

Ink & Ivy

Angela Grey

To the love of my life, Robert,
and our four adult children,
Paige, Cody, Chase, & Brooke,
children-in-law
Vince and Angel,
and grandsons Luke and Logan
—AG

CONTENTS

1 The Ink & Ivy Evening

By the time Marisol Callan locks her drafting laptop and slides the last elevation into a manila folder, her eyes feel crosshatched with lines. The office fluorescents have been humming at a frequency only nerves can hear, and the blueprints have been polite but insistent in their perfection. On the walk over, she tries to blink the ruler-straight out of her vision—past the coffee shop with its clatter of cups, past the florist closing metal buckets over daisy faces, past the rain-polished cobbles that remember a thousand feet. Her shoulders drop one vertebra at a time.

Ink & Ivy waits around the corner as if it has been holding its breath.

The bell above the door gives a content little chime when she turns the key. Inside, lamplight pools like tea in saucers. The old radiators tick softly. Dust floats in the air in a very dignified manner. Books lean toward one another like conspirators in a cozy scandal, and the wallpaper—faded ivy twists on cream—peels back near the register in a curl she has never quite managed to fix. The place smells like cardamom, old paper, and rain in each other's pockets.

Finn pads out from between Memoir and Natural History with the gait of someone who owns the building. He is not a large cat, but he gives the impression of taking up the exact amount of space required by a sovereign entity. Sea-glass eyes. Round face. No tail, just a sturdy rump that wiggles once before he launches himself onto the counter with a soft, authoritative thump.

"Oh, there you are," Marisol says, and her voice comes out softer than she's been all day. "Did you keep an eye on the masses?"

Finn blinks, a slow golden shutter. He makes the tiniest chirrup—approval, or perhaps a list of petty grievances. He smells faintly of cinnamon. Marisol scratches under his chin, and he lifts his face like a priest receiving incense.

"You look like you've been napping in the poetry," she tells him. "Again."

She flicks on two more lamps, checks the till, and sets a kettle to boil on the hot plate beneath the counter. The teacups are stacked like well-behaved planets. Someone—probably the baker from next door—has left a paper bag on the stool. Inside: two scones the size of reasonable dreams. She smiles, breaks one open, and puts a flake on the counter. Finn pretends he doesn't want it until she isn't looking, then neatly steals the entire offering.

They have their evening rhythm, she and the shop and the cat. A kind of choreography learned by repetition until it becomes a ritual. She winds the clock beside the register. She straightens a display of paperbacks no one has been able to leave alone. She switches the sign from CLOSED to OPEN because, despite the hour, people wander in when it rains and the streets are shiny and their lives have edges. Ink & Ivy's hours are more of a suggestion than a fence.

The kettle gives its small, contented song. She pours hot water over a teabag in a mug that says MEASURE TWICE, CUT ONCE and has ink stains in the handle. The first sip unclenches something she didn't realize she'd been holding— something in the ribcage, something behind the eyes. When she exhales, the shop exhales too. She has never said that out loud to anyone; it would sound like fancy. But the walls relax. It is possible.

If she listens—really listens—there's a low sound threaded through the hisses and ticks. Not the building settling, not the skitter of feet overhead in the flat where the landlord's niece sometimes plays violin, not the wind. A murmur. A papery rustle with intent. She told herself the shop breathed after the first week. By the third, she started to answer.

"Evening," she says to the shelves. "We survived Tuesday."

Finn's ear swivels. He jumps from the counter to the poetry ladder, up a rung, down again as if to prove a point about gravity.

Marisol loosens the scarf at her throat and slides the manila folder beneath the counter. The elevations inside belong to a new client downtown—high arches, ambitious glass, a lobby that wants to speak in marble. She likes the work. She is good at it. The geometry of buildings steadies her: the right angles, the rules that do not bend unless you draw them to. But the symmetry has sharp corners. After eight hours of perfect, she needs the soft.

Customers drift in, pulled by rain and lamplight. First, Mr. Chartrand, long coat damp at the hem, spectacles fogged. He has a way of pausing just inside the door, as if checking that his life still fits him.

"Evening, Mr. Chartrand," she says.

"Miss. Callan," he replies, breath hitching like an overexcited book. "Do I smell cardamom?"

"Cardamom and a megalomaniac cat." Finn, on cue, pretends deafness and stretches his paws to the top of a hardback as if massaging it into better character.

Mr. Chartrand removes his hat, shakes a careful halo of raindrops onto the mat, and makes for Poetry with the purposeful sidle of someone approaching an old friend they once offended. He touches the spines as he goes, like counting prayer beads. Marisol watches him out of the corner of her eye. He talks to the books sometimes, quiet as moth wings. She has never interrupted.

Next, the bell rings for someone small and fast: Addison, her backpack wet and her hair pinned haphazardly into a comet tail. She's fifteen and always looks like she's about to apologize to physics. She grins at Marisol with the unapologetic relief of the appointed and beelines for Fantasy.

"I'm not late, right?" she says. "I had to diagram sentences for an hour and a half, and my brain is soup."

"You're exactly on time," Marisol says. "The very idea of sentences would never hold it against you."

Addison snorts and disappears behind a tower of dragon spines. Finn jumps down to follow, tail-less rump bobbing like a punctuation mark. He approves of Addison. He approves of anyone who will read aloud to him from the margins.

The shop fills itself in. The baker comes in to retrieve his paper bag and ends up leaving with a book of sailor's knots and a biography of a woman who mapped the ocean floor. A couple drifts in holding hands, damp laughter catching on their sleeves. A tourist with shoes that were a mistake in this town asks for a postcard and leaves with a hardcover because the cover "feels like bread." The bell, the tea, the soft sibilance of pages turning. The kind of evening that builds a little nest in the sternum.

Between customers, Marisol straightens, sets aside, listens. She knows the particular creak of the mystery shelf, the resigned sigh of Biography, the prim click of New Releases, which has never emotionally recovered from being bumped by a stroller last spring. She knows which step on the back staircase will betray you. She knows the window by Natural History needs propping open with the driftwood the landlord insists is "decorative," and she knows when the wallpaper breathes because of the radiator and when it breathes because it is making up its mind.

She is not sure when she first noticed the other thing. Maybe it was in the first week, and she explained it away as misshelving. Maybe longer. Tonight, it returns, subtle as a hinge.

She's replacing a paperback someone abandoned at the travel table when she sees it: a faint clean rectangle on the shelf in Mythology, as if a book once stood there long enough to keep the dust at bay and then decided to walk out on its own.

"Did you move something?" she asks Finn lightly, casual as tying a shoe.

Finn is on the back of the armchair by the window, front paws tucked under in a position that makes him look like a small, disdainful loaf. He blinks. If there is a book uprising, he intends to be in charge of morale, not logistics.

Marisol rubs her thumb over the outline. The shelf is missing in the bones of her hand. The hum travels up her wrist, a prickle no doctor would find. She glances at the tag on the shelf: MYTHS & FOLKLORE. The books stare back: Tricksters and Sages, The Sea at the Edge of the World, Women Who Breathe Fire, a slim local press chapbook with a woodcut of a fox.

"Strange," she says to the air. To the outline. To the part of her brain that loves when a strange tap politely taps on the glass.

"Do you have any good labyrinths?" Mr. Chartrand calls from the next aisle, as if he can smell philosophy.

"How about Borges?" she says, and plucks a volume with a worn spine that falls open like a mouth. She hands it over. His fingers tremble, some private weather passing.

When she returns to the myth shelf, the clean rectangle is still there. She tries to remember the exact composition of the row. Didn't there used to be a bright green paperback with a stag on the cover? But the memory sloshes, unreliable as a dream in daylight. She reaches out again as if she could feel the missing weight with the pads of her fingers. The shelf's planks are old oak, rubbed smooth by decades: the sort that holds heat and stories.

A draft whispers from somewhere it shouldn't. She follows it to the tall ladder that runs along the Classics section and puts the heels of her hands against the rung, feeling for the little quiver the wood makes when the shop is thinking. It gives a tiny shiver. Finn's head pops up from behind the armchair, ears triangular with interest.

"Don't start," she tells him, but she is smiling, and she knows it.

She climbs halfway up to nudge a stack of epics back into place. As she does, the ladder eases a fraction in its track, left then right, like a sigh. She pauses, one foot up, one foot down, held in the breath between steps. For a heartbeat, the aisle is warmer— as if someone exhaled gently on the small of her back. For a heartbeat, she thinks she hears whispering in a language she doesn't know she knows.

"Are you…?" she begins, softly, to a shelf.

The bell sings the arrival of another customer, and the whisper shies away. She climbs down, cheeks warm, to find a tourist looking for something "local but not too local," which she interprets as witches, lakes, and pie. She sells him a slim novel about a woman who finds an island in her kitchen sink and, because she likes him, a recipe card for berry pie copied from a spiral notebook left behind by a girl who moved away to Iceland and sent postcards of ponies for two years.

An hour passes, then half of one. Outside, the rain relaxes into a drizzle, the streetlight drawing halos on the cobbles. Addison brings three paperbacks to the register and a question about whether a dragon can also be a librarian. ("Obviously," Marisol says, and Finn knocks over a pen for emphasis.) Mr. Chartrand purchases Borges and a book on moss. The baker returns with two slices of cake, and he swears he is not foisting. The shop gathers in the evening like a sweater.

When there is a lull, Marisol wipes the counter with the kind of attention that means she is thinking. She glances toward Mythology again. The empty outline is wider now, as if two books stood there shoulder to shoulder for so long they left their negative photograph behind.

"I don't like that," she murmurs.

Finn hops down from his loft throne and lands without a sound. He crosses the rug with his precise little steps and sits at the base of the myth shelf, staring up, whiskers forward. He does not lift a paw.

He does not blink. He looks, for one ridiculous second, like a sentinel carved from velvet and intent.

She kneels beside him, the rug brushing her knees, the shelf's wood cool against her palm. "What do you see, your majesty?"

He flicks an ear.

She leans closer and—there it is again, the draft. Not from the window. Not from the door. From the seam between two bookcases, where the wallpaper peels just enough to suggest the idea of a secret. She moves the slim chapbook with the fox and finds the seam hidden by its slimness, barely a finger's width, a dark line in the ivy. When she presses her fingertips there, the wood is warm.

A customer coughs politely at the register. The seam cools like a sleeping thing rolling away.

"Coming," Marisol says, and stands, smoothing her skirt, the responsible human again. She rings up a battered travelogue, shows the couple with damp laughter the way the author drew tiny boats when he was happy. By the time she looks back, the clean outline on the shelf is gone. Dust resettled. Books shoulder to shoulder like commuters, insisting they have never met.

She feels the small disappointment of a door that didn't open. Then she reminds herself that there may not have been a door at all.

At closing, she flips the sign, locks the deadbolt, and rests her forehead against the cool pane of the door. The reflections layer themselves: the street, her face, the lamp behind her, Finn's round silhouette on the counter like a moon. In her pocket, her phone buzzes with a message from her boss about a load-bearing wall that is two inches off where it should be. She types a quick reply: Can adjust. Will send the revision tomorrow, and return the phone to her pocket like putting a bird back on a branch.

She turns the lamps down to a low amber hush. The shop settles. In the quiet, she hears it again—not the radiator, not the water in the pipes, not the violin upstairs. A whisper, a rustle, a word just beyond hearing. She doesn't quite catch it. It feels like her name might be on the first page.

"Goodnight, then," she tells the shelves. "Hold together."

Finn jumps to her shoulder without warning, his soft weight a question and an answer. He purrs in her ear with the low, sure thrum of a small engine set for home. She laughs, the kind of laugh she only makes here, and strokes the velvet of one ear. For a moment, the shape of her day rearranges: the sharp-edged office in the morning, the soft-spined evening here, and the thin line of herself walking between them, careful as a tightrope and, maybe, not so careful anymore.

She sets the kettle to drain, washes the mug, and turns the key. Outside, the rain has given up, and the street smells like wet stone. She tucks her scarf close, Finn hops down, and they step into the night.

Behind them, in the pocket of dark where Mythology meets Classics, the seam between the cases sighs. If anyone had been there to see it, they might have thought the wallpaper shifted by the width of a whisper. They might have thought a thin breath of cardamom threaded through where drafts do not go. They might have thought a book—just one—slid a fraction of an inch as if remembering how to move.

But the night is empty now, and the shop is modest, the door locked, and only the shelves know which stories are still awake.

2 Customers & Confidants

By morning, the rain had wrung out the sky and left the town rinsed and blinking. Marisol Callan took the long way to Ink & Ivy, past the square where the farmer's market was dismantling its canvas ribs, past the antique store whose front window had committed to a single cracked teacup as its thesis statement. She carried her drafting tube over one shoulder like a musician pretending not to be in a band. The tube thumped gently against her hip—comforting, utilitarian, a reminder that the part of her brain that measured angles and tolerated building codes could coexist with the part that believed shelves might whisper.

Ink & Ivy was a contented cat in the morning: warm where the radiators purred, bright where the windows drank sunlight. She turned the key, and the bell above the door made the small, dignified sound of good manners. Inside, dust motes conducted an orchestra of light. The shop smelled of paper and that particular sweetness old wood gives off when it has been thinking too long.

Finn appeared on the counter as if summoned by the bell's second syllable. He had the smug look of someone who had done mischief and stored it in a pantry for later.

"Good morning to you, tyrant," Marisol said. "How were the night shifts? Did you make payroll? Negotiate with the wallpaper?"

Finn blinked as if to say that all negotiations had gone in his favor, then stepped forward and pressed his forehead to her chin. The top of his head smelled faintly of cinnamon and the window ledge. He kneaded the ledger book with soft, consequential paws.

"You can't balance the till with your beans," she told him, kissing the air above his ear. "But you can supervise."

He supervised while she did the opening: counted the till, set the kettle on, turned the sign to OPEN, fetched the cardboard box that had arrived yesterday with the neat, slope-shouldered handwriting of a small press in Vermont. As she slit the tape with a butter knife, Finn inserted himself bodily into the lid's trajectory and wedged his whiskers into the scent of cold paper.

"I know, I know," she said. "You're the acquisitions department."

The books inside were bound in linen, the color of unripe pears, with letterpress titles impressed so delicately the words seemed to have been taught to behave. *The*

Almanac of Tidal RooMiss, read the top; *An Essay on Houses That Remember,* the next; then a slim chapbook called *Waubay Insights* with a woodcut of a fox nosing a spoon half-buried in loam. She touched their spines, and the morning rearranged itself around the promise of them.

Finn reached out with one proprietary paw and claimed *Houses That Remember* by laying his paw pad square across the author's name.

"All right," she conceded. "Feature table. You win."

The first customer of the day was Mr. Chartrand, the way first birds claim a branch before the others recall how to wing. He came in with his long coat unbuttoned and the ends of a scarf trailing like punctuation, spectacles slightly askew. He had marrow in his cheeks again today, less of the brittle thinness she'd seen last week. The shop seemed to add color to him as he crossed the threshold.

"Miss. Callan," he said, removing his hat with theatrical humility, as if apologizing to the door for taking up space. "Is it a day for moss?"

"It's always a day for moss," she said. "And I have something else for you—don't chase me out with your hat until you've seen it."

He smiled with half his mouth and put his hat on the hook that rarely held anything but ambitions. Finn hopped to the register, sat like a small judge, and regarded Mr. Chartrand with tolerant fondness. Mr. Chartrand bowed slightly to the cat as if to a bishop.

"I brought back the Pessoa I borrowed," he said, wielding the hardcover as though it were proof of respectable behavior.

"You didn't borrow it, you bought it," Marisol said. "But thank you for pretending we run a lending library on the honor system."

"Don't we?" he said, and the corner of his mouth lifted a little more. She wondered how many times a week he remembered loneliness and chose not to mention it to anyone.

She placed *Houses That Remember* in his hands. "Press out of Vermont," she said. "Essays about buildings that take on the memory of the people who live in them. Kitchens that won't let you forget a recipe. Stairs that keep count. It felt like you."

Mr. Chartrand held the book by its edges, the way you hold a photograph of your grandparents. He ran a thumb over the lettering, then, gently, over the linen, as though smoothing a child's hair. "It does," he said softly. "God help me, it does."

Finn, who considered himself God's regional manager, sniffed the book and, apparently satisfied, allowed it to exist.

Addison arrived ten minutes later, hair exploding in a comet's argument with gravity, a backpack on one shoulder, and a constellation of ink on the back of her left hand. Her eyes brightened at the sight of Finn like someone spotting a rare bird that also did taxes.

"I made it," she said without preamble. "Mrs. Leighton held us hostage while she told a story about diagramming sentences in 1978, and then she tried to diagram her own story, and it was a disaster, and Jenna said—never mind. Hi."

"Hi," Marisol said. "You left a trail of commas behind you."

Addison checked the back of her hand and swiped at one ink blot with her sleeve. "Occupational hazard. Did you get anything new I'm allowed to smell?"

"Actually." Marisol lifted *Waubay Insights* from the box and placed it in Addison's eager hands. "Foxes and spoons."

Addison inhaled dramatically over the paper. "Smells like a meadow that finished high school," she said. "Wait. Is this the press with the little pear books?"

"It is."

Finn planted both forepaws on

Addison's forearm and leaned, as if angling her wrist to the proper reverent angle. She obliged, holding the chapbook the way he preferred, then scratched the velvet line below his ear. He blinked, slow as a tide, and bonked his forehead into her sleeve.

"I was going to the fantasy section," Addison told him, "but if you need me to read about spoons first, I can be flexible."

She disappeared toward the back, Finn trotting after her like a furry exclamation point. A small alarm rang in Marisol—not anxiety, exactly. More like a bell in a far room, muffled by walls, indicating someone had opened a door where doors were not. She ignored it the way you ignore a memory that insists on being an omen.

By noon, the shop had warmed through. The baker from next door leaned over the counter to exchange gossip about a runaway bundt cake and left behind a paper bag that sprouted the smell of lemon. A pair of tourists wandered in looking like the brochure had gotten their angles, asking for "something local without being like, *too* local." Marisol considered this, then handed them a memoir about a woman who ran away to a lighthouse and the light refused to let her go. They left promising to send postcards of their dog from wherever the brochure took them next.

Between customers, the shop moved in small, thoughtful ways. The ladder along Classics shifted an inch to the left when she wasn't looking and then pretended to have strong opinions about being exactly there. The wallpaper swallowed a bubble of air along the seam between Mythology and Classics and then let it go, deflating with a tiny susurration. A paperback on the feature table crept toward the edge as if practicing falling for a stunt, and Finn cured it of that impulse with a paw placed squarely atop the jacket, eyes narrowed in disciplinary concern.

"I forget," Marisol told him, "are you head of security or head of mischief?"

His pupils widened until his eyes were almost all night. He lifted his paw. The paperback slid off the table with a slow flourish and landed on the rug with a sound like a reasonable opinion. Finn looked at her as if to say, *You called my bluff; now we must both live with the consequences.*

"That's what I thought," she said, picking it up.

Mr. Chartrand reappeared at the counter with *Houses That Remember* tucked under his arm and something else in his face—a breeze of worry that traveled the planes of his features and tried to blow out the lamps. "Miss. Callan," he said quietly, and nodded toward the back. "Do your shelves ever...move?"

"They have been known to voice preferences," she said.

"I went to look for that collection of trickster tales— the green paperback with the stag on the cover. I was sure it lived just above the fox chapbook." He touched the air with two fingers where a book would be, which was how some men cross themselves. "But when I reached for it, I...forgot what, precisely, I was reaching for."

Marisol's heart performed that small rabbit hop it did when the world's fabric puckered. "And now?"

"Now I remember that I don't remember." He smiled apologetically. "Which is not the useful end of memory."

She led him back to Mythology. Addison sat perched on the arm of the leather chair by the window, one knee up, *Waubay Insights* open in her lap. Finn had claimed the seat itself and sprawled like a velvet flood, chin propped on the arm, one paw extended in ecstatic ownership. Addison read aloud to him in a murmur like river stones, and he vibrated gently, purr audible as a small machine building a bridge in the chest.

"...and the fox said, 'I will dig where the ground is soft with forgetting, and you will eat with the spoon made of my memory.'"

Addison looked up as they approached. "Is that weird or is it good-weird?"

"Both," Marisol said. "Which is the correct ratio?"

She crouched in front of the shelf. The line of books in Mythology had their earnest faces on: *Tricksters and Sages*, *The Sea at the Edge of the World*, *Women Who Breathe Fire*, a slim anthology of river myths with a blue thread marker peeking like a tongue. Everything looked convincing as it should be. But close up, she could see what Mr. Chartrand meant. There was a fraction too much air between *Tricksters and Sages* and the river anthology, as if a slender body had just exited the crowd. Dust gathered in a low tide line along the shelf plank—but there, a clean oval where a thumb might have smudged it yesterday. She put her own thumb there. The wood was warm in the way old wood is warm: heat remembered, not radiated.

"Maybe it's in Folkways?" she said, standing, trying on normal like a cardigan that didn't quite fit. "Or mis-shelved with Nature? Stags sometimes get ambitious."

"I'll check," Mr. Chartrand said. His smile had the sweetness of someone protecting her from something by pretending to be silly. He wandered off.

Addison closed the chapbook and wedged one finger between its pages to hold the place. "Okay," she said in the tone of someone recapping a soap opera. "So either your shelves are hungry and ate a book, or someone borrowed it and decided to ghost us, or the book read itself so hard it ascended."

Finn rose with the solemnity of a man knighted against his will and leapt to the low table. He sniffed the seam where the ivy wallpaper peeled back a finger's width between the myth case and Classics. The whiskers on his left cheek quivered as if trying out a word. He touched the seam with his nose, then looked at Marisol with an expression she'd come to recognize as *Pay attention without making a scene.*

She knelt again and did not press this time. She just put her hand flat on the wood beside the seam and let her palm learn the temperature, the grain, the patient heartbeat of a building listening to itself be a building. The faintest breath of cool air slid across her knuckles, not from the window, not from the door. From here. From where there should not be anywhere.

"Do you feel that?" she whispered.

Addie slid off the chair and crouched, eyes wide, the comet of her hair spilling into her field of wonder. She held her hand an inch above the seam, then brought it down until her skin touched the wallpaper. "Oh," she said, soft as a match taken into confidence. "It's like...when you press your ear to a shell and hear all your neighbors."

Finn extended a paw and touched the wallpaper once, gently. The paper did not move. Or it did, but in the way leaves move when they decide not to.

A customer coughed politely at the counter. The cough was resolutely human, and with it the spell folded itself, tidy as a receipt. Marisol stood and brushed her knees, which were now obliged to be ordinary. "Duty calls," she said, and they smiled at each other, a conspiracy made of nothing, a promise made of maybe.

At the register, a woman with a tote bag printed with aggressive sunflowers wanted a birthday recommendation for a man who liked maps and pies and women who made his life difficult in ways that later turned out to be educational. Marisol found her a memoir and a novel and, because the universe enjoys symmetry, the small press atlas of imaginary towns that always made people cry on page forty-three. While she wrapped the books in brown paper, Finn supervised the string with such intensity that his whiskers were vertical. When the knot was secure, he pressed a paw to it to test the integrity of her bow, then allowed the purchase to proceed.

The day wore on, making itself a quilt out of small squares: a grandmother buying a book of ghost stories "for me, of course," a boy with a coin jar counting out exactly enough for a paperback about a clever dog, a woman in a raincoat who asked for a book with a perfect last line and left with three. Finn intercepted a rogue housefly with the dexterity of a seasoned swordsman and paraded his victory around the Poetry section like a spoil of war before becoming distracted by a sunbeam and sprawling there as though he had invented light.

In the quiet hour between the afternoon rush and the schoolkids pouring in to be saved by indoor places, Addison drifted back to the counter, *Waubay Insights* now bristling with the small, torn paper flags she used instead of a pencil.

"So," she said. "Hypothesis time."

"Always my favorite time," Marisol said, sliding a biscuit across the counter in the manner of a bartender who had been tipped in stories. "Shoot."

Addie snapped her fingers for Finn's attention. He opened one eye, considered the merits of participation, and closed it again with serene contempt for the premise of effort. "If the shelves are like...not alive-alive, but like...*house alive,* then maybe the missing book wasn't stolen. Maybe it was...moved."

"Where?" Marisol said.

"Closer to whatever it's listening to," Addison said, then squinted, as though the thought had looked better in her head before it came out into the air and saw itself. "I don't know. Or maybe it's like matching socks. You know how you lose one in the dryer and you think you've been punished for hubris, but then you find it months later inside a fitted sheet? Books are socks. The shelf is a sheet. That metaphor got away from me."

"It had potential," Marisol said, serious as glass. "Also, the dryer is a known portal."

Addison grinned, grateful for being taken seriously where she might have been teased elsewhere. "Do you ever—like—*hear* the shop?"

Marisol glanced toward Mythology and then back at Addie, as if the shelves might take offense at being discussed like weather. "Sometimes," she said. "Mostly I feel it. When something is out of place. When someone needs a book that they didn't know existed. When the wallpaper wants to be a wall."

Addison nodded. "Me too. I mean, not here. At home. My mom's recipe box remembers my grandmother in a way that makes the whole kitchen smell like nutmeg when I open it. My mom laughs and says it's in my head." She looked at Finn, who was carefully placing one paw over his nose. "I don't think it is."

Marisol looked down at her hands, ink-stained from receipts, dry from paper, steady by habit. "Blueprints are just ways of believing in a building before it exists," she said, surprising herself. "You draw the lines as if the walls will come when you call them, and then they do."

Addison considered that, cheeks dimpling with thought. "So maybe stories are like that too."

Finn made a small, decisive sound in his sleep that might have been agreement or a declaration of sovereignty.

The bell over the door chimed at half-past four; a gust of cooler air followed a man in a pale coat whose shoes did not appear to accept that the town had puddles. He paused to glance up at the bell as if it had stated his name incorrectly, then took in the shop with a look that was not curiosity so much as inventory. His eyes were a light color and did not seem to change when he smiled.

"Welcome," Marisol said, reflex smoothing her voice. "Let me know if you need a hand."

"Thank you," he said. His voice had a polite ribbon running through it, the kind you keep because it might be useful later and then never find again. "I'm searching for something particular."

He moved along the shelves without picking anything up, only letting his gaze skim the spines as though reading by osmosis. When he reached the feature table, he paused at *The Almanac of Tidal RooMiss*, then smiled as if he'd made a private joke at the book's expense and set it askew with one finger. Finn woke. Finn watched. Finn did not blink.

Addison, suddenly intent on the price sticker of a bookmark, rolled it between finger and thumb and did not look up.

The man returned to the counter as if he'd been here many times and placed no books upon it. "I'm looking," he said pleasantly, "for a volume called *The Almanac of Autumn Winds*. You must have it."

Marisol felt the small slip of the world under her feet, the way a rug sneaks a joke into a room by moving half an inch. She kept her face somewhere between tea and lamp. "I don't think I know that one," she said. "Autumn winds, you said? Sounds lovely."

"It is," he said. "It knows the names of the months in languages no one speaks anymore." He looked at Finn, who had swelled quietly to twice his arrogance. "Charming animal."

"Unionized," Marisol said.

"Mm," the man said, as if she'd confessed to an unfashionable vice. "You'll look for the almanac."

It wasn't a question. It was the sound of a chair pulled out without waiting to be invited to sit. Politeness, sharpened.

"I'll check our system," Marisol said, trying to keep the temperature from changing. She tapped the keys with more purpose than faith. The search returned several almanacs (gardening, celestial events, *tidal rooms*), none claiming autumn winds. She opened the distributor portal, which was like asking an oracle who also sold packing tape. Nothing. "It might be out of print."

"Nothing is ever out of print," he said, and smiled the wrong amount. "Some things are simply...no longer required."

Finn stood. He did not raise his fur, did not growl. He placed one paw on the counter and extended his claws, not as a threat but as the punctuation to a sentence he intended to speak later. The man's gaze slid over the paw the way oil slides over water and refuses to mix.

"If it arrives," the man said, "I'll come back for it. I'm sure you'll know it when you see it." He placed a business card on the counter that had nothing on it but a name that didn't look like a name and a phone number too orderly to be believed.

"Pleasure." He left without buying anything, and the bell said his exit as politely as it could.

Addison released a breath, the way you release a kite string when you realize you have accidentally caught a hawk. "I did not care for that," she said.

"Nor did I," Mr. Chartrand said from the biography aisle, where he stood very still, as though refusing to frighten whatever might be standing behind him. "He looked at the books like he hated their ability to be more than one thing at once."

Marisol slipped the card into the drawer and closed it with a decisive little snick. "We don't have what he wants," she said, and Finn, who rarely condescended to such simple gestures, nodded.

The remaining afternoon went about its business, though with the cautious corners you use when you suspect someone has rearranged the knives. After closing, Addison gathered her things and made Finn submit to a farewell nose kiss. He endured with the dignity of a monarch, permitting rural customs.

"Text me if your wallpaper opens a portal," Addie said, shouldering her backpack.

"I don't have your number," Marisol said.

Addison blinked, then grinned like someone catching up with her own life. "Right. Here." They exchanged numbers over the counter, for reasons neither of them stated but both understood as necessary in a vocabulary older than cell towers. Mr. Chartrand, already in his coat, pretended to be very interested in the corkboard posting for the book club that mostly argued about cake.

When the bell had said its last goodnight and the street poured itself into evening, Marisol turned the sign and locked the door. The shop exhaled in the manner of a place that has put on its slippers. She made tea because her hands wanted something to do that wasn't thinking about the card in the drawer or the seam in the wallpaper or the way the word *almanac* had sounded as it came out of the man's mouth—like something being moved two inches left of where it should be.

Finn leapt to the counter, landing with the practiced grace of a cat who had rehearsed the move a thousand times. His paws spread like soft punctuation marks, his whiskers twitching as if in approval of the evening's turnout. He gave a decisive trill and, without waiting for permission, curled himself around the credit card machine, his fur already shedding a halo of fine hairs that would cling to receipts and sleeves for days.

"Finn," Marisol sighed, flicking a stray tuft from the cash drawer, "customers don't want to take you home in *that* way."

Finn yawned, revealing a flash of pink tongue, and deliberately knocked a pen into the tip jar.

The bell above the door jingled, and in shuffled Mr. Chartrand. His coat smelled faintly of rain and pipe tobacco, and his hair—what remained of it—was a soft white crown that always seemed to catch the lamplight just so. He removed his hat with ceremony and tipped it toward Finn first, as though acknowledging the true proprietor.

"Good evening, your highness," he said gravely to the cat.

Finn accepted this homage with a blink so slow it might have been mistaken for a benediction.

Marisol chuckled. "I see where I rank."

"You, my dear, rank just below royalty," Mr. Chartrand said, adjusting his spectacles. "But don't take it personally. None of us competes with cats. Or books, for that matter."

"Fair enough," she said, pouring hot water over a fresh teabag. "The usual?"

"Something with teeth," he replied, as he always did, which meant poetry.

While he drifted toward the tall shelves

that seemed to lean closer when he approached, the bell rang again, brighter this time. Addie burst in like a dropped stack of papers—quick, unpredictable, edges everywhere. Her sneakers squeaked on the mat, and her backpack slumped to one side, heavy with secrets and overdue homework.

"Miss. Callan!" she said, cheeks flushed from the damp. "Tell me you got the new shipment. Please, please, *please*."

Marisol tilted her head. "Depends. What's the magic word?"

"Dragon," Addison said without hesitation.

Finn stretched across the counter and tapped the register with his paw, as if stamping approval.

"Fine," Marisol said, hiding a smile. She slid a fresh fantasy paperback across the counter, the cover awash with mountains and a sword too large to be practical. "Straight from the box."

Addie gasped, clutching it like treasure. "I knew it! You're the best."

"I'll remind you of that when you forget your bookmark and dog-ear the pages," Marisol teased.

Addison grinned guiltily, already drifting toward her usual armchair, Finn trotting after her like a librarian on patrol. He hopped up onto the armrest, curled into a loaf, and pretended not to notice her stroking his fur while she cracked open the first chapter.

The shop warmed with their presence. Mr. Chartrand muttered lines of poetry to himself, his voice a hush of worn leather. Addison's page-turns sounded like small applause. The rain tapped politely at the windows. Marisol sipped her tea, listening to the low chorus of comfort.

When the baker from next door popped in, bearing a tray of experimental ginger cookies, Finn abandoned Addie without a shred of remorse and stationed himself at the baker's feet. He meowed once, sharp and imperious.

"Honestly," Marisol muttered, watching the baker laugh as he crumbled a cookie into Finn's waiting mouth. "He'll trade loyalty for pastry any day."

The cat chewed delicately, eyes closing in bliss. Then, as if sensing Marisol's disapproval, he leapt back onto the counter, crumbs dusting his whiskers. He sat upright, regal as a portrait, and fixed her with an unrepentant stare.

"You're impossible," she said. But she couldn't stop the smile tugging at her lips.

For a moment, Ink & Ivy seemed to glow—not from the lamps, but from the quiet harmony of its inhabitants: the professor murmuring to verse, the teenager lost in dragons, the baker licking sugar from his thumb, the books breathing softly on their shelves, and a cat who ruled it all with crumbs in his whiskers and mischief in his eyes.

Mr. Chartrand had claimed his usual chair beneath the high shelves, his hat resting on his knee and his glasses perched at an angle that would have horrified any optometrist. He recited a line of Neruda under his breath, savoring the syllables the way other men savored wine.

Addison sprawled in her corner armchair, legs draped over one side, already three chapters deep in her new dragon saga. Finn had stationed himself on the back of her chair again, a furry gargoyle, every so often leaning down to inspect the pages with what looked suspiciously like judgment.

"You can't read yet," Addie whispered to him, giving his ear a scratch. "Or can you?"

Finn answered with a single sneeze, then leapt away to make his rounds.

Marisol followed him with her eyes, amused. "I think he reads when no one's watching."

The baker chuckled, setting down the tray of ginger cookies on the counter. "That cat's too clever by half. Wouldn't surprise me one bit if he starts running story hour."

"Don't encourage him," Marisol said, breaking a cookie in two and slipping the smaller piece onto a napkin for Finn. He accepted it with the dignity of a monarch receiving tribute, crumbs sticking to his whiskers.

The bell above the door chimed again, gentler this time, and Mrs. Marquel shuffled in. Her umbrella dripped a trail across the floor, but she always smelled of lilacs, even in the rain. She made a beeline for Gardening, as she always did, muttering about the state of her roses.

"Evening, Mrs. Marquel," Marisol called.

"Evening, dear," came the distracted reply. "Do you have anything new on composting? Mine's too wet, and the neighbors are starting to complain."

"I'll check in the back," Marisol said, though she knew exactly which title would soothe her.

While she searched, Finn hopped down and escorted Mrs. Marquel like a dutiful shop assistant, weaving between her ankles. He rubbed once against her shin, then darted toward the counter again, triumphant as if he'd helped her find the right shelf.

When Marisol returned with a thin paperback, Mrs. Marquel smiled. "Always the perfect book, thank you. And Finn, of course."

The cat purred loudly, basking in the compliment.

By the time the hour wound on, the shop had settled into its favorite state: not bustling, not empty, but comfortably full. Mr. Chartrand scribbled notes in a battered journal, murmuring, "Ah, yes, that's it." Addison giggled at something her dragon protagonist said aloud, as if sharing a joke with Finn. Mrs. Marquel flipped through composting advice, nodding firmly at each page. The baker returned to fetch his tray, only to linger, talking about how the scent of books reminded him of his grandmother's kitchen.

Marisol poured herself another cup of tea, savoring the way the warmth traveled all the way down. This—this hush of lamplight, rain tapping on the glass, voices low and content, the rustle of pages—was what made the long drafting days worthwhile. Buildings might stand tall and symmetrical, but here was where she felt life tilted its head and smiled.

Finn leapt back to the counter, crumbs still clinging to his whiskers. He sat, tail-less and perfectly at ease, and gave a small, imperious meow.

"Yes, yes," Marisol said, scratching under his chin. "You run the place. I'm just your assistant."

The cat closed his eyes, purring so loudly the counter vibrated. The customers chuckled softly, the shelves seemed to sigh in contentment, and Marisol thought that if all nights could be like this, she wouldn't ask for more.

By the time the last cookie crumb was swept into a napkin and Mrs. Marquel's umbrella had tapped its farewell on the cobblestones, Ink & Ivy settled into its evening hush. The rain had dwindled to a mist, and the windows fogged from the warmth inside. Marisol flipped the sign to CLOSED, the bell giving a final polite chime as if it too were ready for bed.

Mr. Chartrand tucked his books beneath his arm, bowed once to Finn, and disappeared into the drizzle. Addison lingered a moment longer, hugging her paperback like it was a lantern.

"You'll tell me if more of these come in, right?" she asked.

"Always," Marisol promised.

Addison grinned, pushed her hair from her face, and darted into the night, sneakers squeaking on wet pavement.

The bell stilled. The shop exhaled.

Marisol leaned against the counter, her teacup cooling in her hands. "Well," she said softly, "we survived another Tuesday."

Finn padded across the counter,

brushing against her sleeve. He butted his head under her chin until she laughed.

"You're shameless," she told him, scooping him up. His round body fit perfectly against her chest, purr rumbling like a far-off train. She carried him as she dimmed the lamps, one by one, until the shop was a patchwork of golden pools and deep, comfortable shadow.

Together, they made the last rounds. She checked that the back door was locked, that the kettle was unplugged, and that the display by the window looked inviting for tomorrow. Finn leapt from her arms to inspect a low shelf, then followed her back to the counter with a trill that sounded like a job well done.

When everything was in order, Marisol paused in the center of the shop. The shelves stood tall and watchful, their spines glimmering faintly in the lamplight. It was quiet, but not empty, the kind of quiet that hummed with companionship.

"You know," she whispered to Finn, "if I could, I'd stay here all night. Just you, me, and the books."

Finn purred louder, curling around her ankles, and for a moment she could almost believe he understood every word.

She gathered her scarf, slipped her bag over her shoulder, and turned the key in the front door. The lock clicked with finality, and in the reflection of the glass, she saw herself, Finn's silhouette at her feet, and the soft glow of Ink & Ivy behind them.

"Goodnight, little kingdom," she murmured.

The shelves gave no reply, but the silence felt approving. With Finn trotting beside her, Marisol stepped into the damp night, the scent of lilacs and cardamom trailing after her like a blessing.

3 The Vanishing Mythologies

By late afternoon the next day, the sky had wrung itself dry. Puddles held small versions of the town, streetlamps wearing halos that would brighten when evening finally slipped its key into the lock. Marisol Callan walked the last block to Ink & Ivy with a rolled set of elevations tucked under her arm and Finn's favorite treats in her pocket, a peace offering for having stayed at the drafting office longer than she meant to.

The bell over the door chimed hello. The shop greeted her with lamplight and the warm, faint spice of yesterday's cardamom, as if no hour had passed since she'd whispered goodnight. Finn appeared from between Biography and Travel with the slow, assured gait of a small monarch. He hopped to the counter, accepted a treat with offended dignity—as though she owed him interest—and rubbed his cheek against her wrist.

"I know," she said, setting her plans beneath the counter. "You had to run the kingdom alone. Tragic."

Finn trilled, then rearranged himself across the receipt printer so completely that any future commerce would require negotiation.

"Move," she said.

He did not. Marisol slid the printer three inches to the left, and Finn slid with it, a furry paperweight with convictions.

By the time she'd turned on the kettle, Mr. Chartrand pushed through the door, the damp wool of his coat smelling pleasantly of a walk taken without hurry. He tipped his hat to Finn first, as he always did. "Your Majesty. Miss. Callan."

"Evening. Poetry's been dusting itself in anticipation," Marisol said, handing him a mug he never refused. "Something with teeth?"

He smiled. "And moss."

"Teeth and moss it is."

Addison burst in behind him with a gust of street air and the perpetual sense that gravity was a suggestion she chose to ignore. Her backpack hung off one shoulder; a sprig of something green poked from a pocket.

"Miss. Callan! You will not believe how chapter six ends." She flung herself toward her chair, then stopped to bury her fingers in Finn's neck fur. "Hi, boss."

Finn allowed the scritches with the expression of a deity humoring worship.

The evening stretched itself into the shape they all liked best. The baker popped in with a paper bag and a new theory about cardamom. Mrs. Marquel arrived smelling of lilac and rain, fretting over her compost and her neighbor's opinions. Marisol found the exact booklet to soothe both and rang it up while Finn stationed himself on the mat by the door like a concierge.

"It's the way he sits," the baker said, watching Finn appraise a new arrival. "As if he's counting how many pies I owe him."

"You do owe him," Marisol said. "And me."

The baker put two ginger cookies on a napkin as penance. Finn devoured his half with surgical precision and then made a circuit of the room, greeting ankles and auditing armchairs. Marisol poured tea for whoever looked like they needed it, swapped out a burned-out bulb, and restacked a tower of paperbacks that loved collapsing on principle.

At some point between Mrs. Marquel's lecture on worms and Addison's gasp over a plot twist, Marisol noticed it: a small, clean rectangle on a middle shelf of Mythology where dust hadn't settled. She paused, mind snagging on the neatness of it. Yesterday, she'd been sure she'd seen a gap; last night, she'd told herself she'd imagined it. Now the gap had companions.

She watched the counter, made change, and laughed at a joke about moss with Mr. Chartrand. Then she drifted toward Mythology with her tea in hand, casual as a yawn.

Myths & Folklore spanned two long cases, old oak, shelves bowed with use. The top shelves wore the big, showy hardcovers with gilt titles and ribbon markers. The middle ran wide with paperbacks that had passed through many hands: tricksters and saints, islands that moved when you looked away, a regional collection of lake ghosts with a cover so lurid it dared you to love it. The bottom held slim chapbooks from local presses, stapled spines and woodcuts, and poems that knew the taste of winter.

Tonight, in the middle, a book-shaped absence sat like a missing tooth. And six inches to the right—another. Above them—another. If she squinted, they made a pattern, as if someone had plucked stones from a wall.

Marisol set her mug on the ladder's lowest rung and ran a finger along one clean outline. The oak was warm, as if a hand had been there a moment ago. She swallowed.

Finn arrived without sound and planted himself at her heel, looking up where she looked. His whiskers, which had been careless all evening, went forward with interest. He lifted one paw, slowly, and tapped the empty space. His paw met wood; he withdrew it and flicked his ear, annoyed.

"Do you remember what sat here?" she

asked him, because it was easier than asking herself.

Finn's pupils widened. He didn't blink.

"Miss. Callan?" Addison called from the armchair. "Do you still have that little book of lake myths, the one with the red canoe on the cover? My friend wants to borrow it after me, and I promised I'd—"

Her voice stalled when she reached the end of the aisle and saw Marisol kneeling by the shelf.

"What's wrong?"

Marisol forced her shoulders down from around her ears. "I'm... trying to find something."

"The canoe one?" Addison stepped closer, peering at the spines. "It lived right... here." She tapped the air a cautious inch above the shelf. The precise spot where one of the clean outlines sat. "Huh."

Mr. Chartrand appeared like a moth drawn to a good question, cradling his poetry. "What are we finding that isn't there?"

"The lake myths," Addison said. "And maybe something else."

Mr. Chartrand bent, spectacles sliding unhelpfully down his nose. He touched the dustless rectangle with two fingers, then frowned. "Neat."

"As in tidy," Marisol said, "not good."

He made a thoughtful sound and straightened with care. "I do recall a canoe," he said slowly. "Red. I read the first story—something about a fisherman who was also a... what was it? Ferryman? Fox? Those consonants are conspirators." He rubbed his temple, mildly irritated with his brain. "Ah. No matter. It was here."

"Was?" Addison said. "Or is?"

Marisol pulled back, sat on her heels, and let her eyes go soft, the way she did when she was trying to see a building's lines before they were drawn. The shelves blurred—the forest before the individual trees. The clean outlines resolved into a quiet geometry: every third space, a gap. A rhythm if you listened with your eyes.

She rose, rolled her shoulders, and slid two neighboring books apart, giving the shelf a gentle shake in case a fallen volume surprised her by leaping to its feet. Nothing. Just the comfortable huff of old wood.

Behind her, the bell rang, and the baker stuck his head in again, halfway to an apology for forgetting his tray, halfway to a new rumor about cinnamon. He saw her expression and shut his mouth on the rumor.

"What happened?"

"Nothing," Marisol said too quickly, then softened her voice. "Maybe nothing. A few...

titles might be mis-shelved."

Finn jumped onto the ladder rung and up again, a compact coil of muscle and decision. He pranced along the rung until he could press his cheek against the shelf at eye level, then he opened his mouth slightly, tasting the air the way cats did when something needed decoding. His whiskers trembled. He bumped his head against the seam where the two bookcases met.

"Finn," she said, an edge of warning that was mostly worry.

He bumped the seam again and looked back over his shoulder at her. It was not a casual glance. It was a look she had come to read as: Pay attention. Then he butted the seam once more, harder, and the tiniest tremor shivered through the oak.

Addison gasped. "Did you see—?"

"It's an old case," Mr. Chartrand began, rational and kind.

But Marisol had already put her palm to the seam. Warmth. A thin, steady hum, not in the air but under her skin, like the shop had a pulse in its wood. The hum threaded up her wrist and into the small bones of her hand. The back of her neck prickled.

For half a breath, she heard something. Not language; not the radiator; not a mouse. The sound of a page turned by someone who did not want to be heard.

She closed her eyes. The hum matched her heartbeat for three beats and then faded, as if embarrassed to be caught.

When she opened her eyes, Finn had positioned himself between her and the seam, a low, vibrating rumble in his chest that was neither purr nor growl but some third thing reserved for serious business. He planted his feet. He did not blink.

Addison whispered, "That's his 'don't' noise."

"Don't what?" the baker asked.

Finn held his ground. The ladder rung creaked a small warning under his weight; he did not care.

Marisol withdrew her hand. The warmth dissipated like breath on a mirror when the room cools. The dustless rectangles did not refill with books. The row looked almost normal now, if you didn't know where to look.

She became aware, abruptly, of everyone's faces turned toward her: Addie bright and worried, Mr. Chartrand intent, the baker hanging in the doorway with an armful of paper bags, Mrs. Marquel craning from Gardening with her compost treatise pressed to her chest. It was a gentle, familiar audience, one that wished her nothing but tea and solutions.

"It's probably me," she said, and the lie

tasted like a chipped cup. "Long day at the office. I might have reshelved something without thinking. I'll do a proper search after closing."

Addison looked like she wanted to argue with physics again. Mr. Chartrand adjusted his glasses and, with a tact so deft it was its own kind of love, said, "I'll check Folklore. One never knows where the mischievous will sneak."

"Mischievous composters," Mrs. Marquel muttered, and turned a page pointedly.

The room eased back into its evening, but with a new angle—the way chatter at a dinner party drops half a note after a glass shatters in another room. People went on doing what they were doing. Marisol went through the motions of cashiering, answering, pouring, and smiling. Finn shadowed her, shoulder to ankle, a silent metronome.

When the door finally chimed on the last goodbye, the shop's quiet came down like a shawl. Marisol flipped the sign, locked the bolt, and stood in the central aisle without moving. The lamplight pooled on the rugs; the ivy wallpaper held its own breath. She set the kettle to boil and didn't make tea.

"All right," she said softly, to the shelves,

to herself, to the seam. "Let's look."

She took every book in Myths & Folklore off every shelf, one by one. Finn supervised from the ladder, pupils wide, tail stub twitching in brief, emphatic punctuation. She stacked books in tidy towers by topic, by region, by color when her hands wanted the comfort of order. She counted the slots where dust hadn't settled and wrote the number on a ticket stub. She listened for the hum and heard only the tick of hot metal cooling on the kettle.

By the time she had a sweating glass of water instead of tea and six towers of paperbacks within easy tipping distance, she knew three things: first, the canoe book was not anywhere it could reasonably be; second, six other books were gone with it; third, she could not say their titles out loud, though the shapes of their covers ghosted under her eyelids when she closed her eyes.

She sat on the floor among the towers and pressed her thumb to the place on the seam where the warmth had been. The wood felt like wood. Beneath it, the wall felt like a wall. Her own pulse was the only thing knocking.

Finn leapt down and threaded himself into her lap, a heavy loaf pinning her to the moment. He tilted his head and looked up at her with a seriousness that stole a breath.

"I see it too," she told him. Saying it made her feel both better and more alarmed. "I just don't know what I'm seeing."

Finn blinked once, slow, the universal feline benediction. Then he turned, stood with his front paws braced on her thigh, and stretched toward the seam again, nose almost touching the ivy-printed paper. He sniffed, held still, and, just once, huffed a soft sound that might have been a cat's version of a no.

"All right," she said again, to him this time. "We'll leave the seam alone."

She rebuilt the section with careful hands, leaving small slips of paper where the books should have been—blank except for a sketched rectangle and a question mark in the corner. It looked foolish, and it made her feel less so. When she replaced the last paperback and stepped back, the shelves were as they had been, minus the missing. The towers became rows, the towers became order, the towers became a place a person could breathe again.

At closing, she dimmed the lamps until the shop was a honeycomb of warm squares. She washed the mug she hadn't used and dried it for the comfort of doing a thing that had a beginning, a middle, and an end. She checked the back door twice. She stood once more in front of the seam and did nothing, which was harder than anything else she'd done all day.

"Goodnight, little kingdom," she whispered, voice rougher than she meant. "Hold together."

Finn jumped to her shoulder in a single, practiced motion, all heat and soft weight, and pressed his cheek against her jaw. His purr rolled through her like a small engine deciding to carry them both home. She set her palm flat on the nearest shelf for one heartbeat more.

If the oak warmed under her hand, it did so politely and without witness.

She turned the key. Outside, the puddles had gone black and glassy, the town wearing its evening face. Finn hopped down to heel her, and they stepped into the street together.

Behind them, in the narrow breath of space where Mythology met Classics, the dust settled. A slip of paper she'd tucked as a placeholder lifted the smallest corner, as if a draft had remembered itself. Then it lay flat again, quiet as a kept secret.

4 The Whispering Blueprints

Marisol Callan's apartment always smelled faintly of pencil shavings and oranges. The oranges, because she bought them by the bag and forgot to eat them in a timely way, so bowls of them glowed like small suns on every flat surface; the pencil shavings, because she still preferred the quiet ache of a sharpened lead to the drama of a mechanical click. Tonight, the scent was joined by damp wool and the metallic sweetness that follows rain. She set her satchel on the entry table, kicked off her shoes by accident and on purpose, and dropped her keys into the ceramic dish shaped like a leaf that her aunt insisted brought good luck.

Finn trotted in ahead of her—he always got there first somehow—leapt onto the back of the couch, and executed a clean, theatrical flop that conveyed both exhaustion and superiority. He tucked his front paws beneath him, becoming a perfect loaf. His eyes half-closed. His whiskers flicked at something only he could see.

"Don't pretend you didn't sleep through ninety percent of the day," Marisol said, flipping on a lamp. Light poured across the small living room she loved precisely because it had been several rooms in a former life; the ceiling dipped where a wall used to be, and everything skewed gently, like a smile that didn't quite behave. "You're the only employee who takes a nap break during rush."

Finn answered with a trill that could have meant anything from Try me to I unionized.

She carried a glass of water to her drafting table—the battered oak one she'd found in a salvage yard and fallen for like a person. It lived by the window where streetlight pooled in rectangles and the radiator clicked companionably in the colder months. Tonight, she pulled the blinds halfway and opened the window a slim inch to let in a thread of cool air and the low, tire-soft wash of distant traffic. The table's surface was a map of her habits: faint graphite ghosts, divots where compasses had pressed too hard, a thumb-smudge constellation that didn't line up with any known sky.

Her phone buzzed. She glanced at the screen.

ISLEY: You're a saint if you can reroute that load-bearing wall tonight. New clients are having an opinion flare-up. I'll owe you coffee for a week.

She smiled despite herself. Isley had a way of making emergencies sound like a minor weather report and debt sound delicious. She typed back:

MARISOL: Consider it rerouted. I was going to draw anyway.

ISLEY: You're the best. Also, you left your lucky scale in Studio B.

MARISOL: Borrow it. Don't anger it.

ISLEY: Never.

She set the phone face down. On the table: the rolled set of elevations from the clerk's desk downstairs, the site plan she'd carried with her in case inspiration occurred inside a bag, her favorite 2H pencil, a kneaded eraser the size of a small potato, a compass scuffed to a dull shine, a triangular scale with the paint worn off the 1/8 inch side. She anchored the corners of her vellum with smooth stones she'd pocketed from the lake last summer, each one the exact weight to persuade paper to behave.

"Okay, little wall," she told the drawing, clicking on the task lamp. Its circle of light parted the room from the rest of the night. "Two inches left without breaking your back. We can do that."

Finn flowed off the couch without unfolding—one minute loaf, the next minute a pouring of cat—and hopped onto the table. He sniffed the stones, bumped his head on the lamp, and wound himself around the pencil cup until it made a complaining sound.

"You can sit," Marisol said. "But you cannot sit there." She moved him gently from the center of the vellum to the far corner of the table, where a cat bed waited, tufted with stolen sweater fluff and the soft despair of lint rollers. He refused the bed and chose the vellum's corner anyway, arranging himself like a paperweight with opinions.

"Fine." She set the tip of the pencil to the paper and breathed the way she did right before the first line—the inhale, the pause, the feeling of stepping into the blank. Then she drew.

The lines came easily at first: existing grid, roof parapet, the course of HVAC like a sentence that knew where it was going. She lost herself the way she liked to—stroke and lift, rotate the vellum, lift and stroke, adjust the parallel bar, sight along the edge of the triangle, check the scale against the habit of her hand. Outside the window, the town's square lights settled into their night shapes. Somewhere, a siren rose and fell, a small, sad song for a car alarm or something more human. Finn kneaded the corner he'd stolen, purring like a machine set to low.

And then—quietly, like a person entering a library—the drawing began to stop being the drawing.

It didn't happen all at once, no neat

cinematic ripple. It was instead a refusal of the pencil to obey the logic of the plan. Her wall, instead of bending around a stairwell, leaned toward a shelf-shaped gesture—three long strokes and a smaller one to the left, like an aisle with a soft knee. She frowned, erased, redrew. The line slid, persuasive as a hand on your elbow at a dance, until it clicked into an angle that did not belong to a lobby...but belonged, with a familiarity so intimate it felt like an ache, to the second row in Ink & Ivy's Myths & Folklore.

She set the pencil down and flexed her fingers. Her stomach made the quiet memory of tea.

"Don't do this," she told herself. Then, because honesty sometimes worked better than sternness, she added, "Do what?"

Finn lifted his head. He stared at the paper; he stared at her. His ears went forward in the keen way they had when he was listening not to sound but to gusto.

"Fine," she said to the cat and also to the sore want in her chest. "Two inches left can wait."

She pulled a fresh sheet of tracing paper, floated it over the plan, and taped it down lightly. Instead of fighting the line that wanted to be a shelf, she chased it. Pencil point, whisper-soft, she drew the aisle the way her feet knew it: the mild skew where the floor's old boards pushed the ladder track half a degree off square; the thin dip where too many readers had leaned too hard against a favorite section; the uprise at the end where the shelf met the case seam by the climbing ivy. Her hand didn't falter. The graphite darkened where muscle memory asked for it. Under her pencil, the table stopped being a table. The room stopped being a room. The drawing cleared its throat and asked very politely to be a map.

She added the neighboring cases by instinct and habit until a shape revealed itself—a bloom and declension, something like a nautilus if a nautilus were made of wood and spines and tiny slips of paper with prices in pencil. She paused, lifted the pencil, and let the ache do the deciding. Where— exactly where—had the empty rectangles been?

Her hand hovered, then landed. There, and there, and there, every third place in a soft diagonal that, if extended, would pass through the seam where she had felt warmth. Her pencil marked each missing— small squares, open, a notation her body recognized as "incomplete" even without trying.

The lamp hummed. The radiator ticked. Finn's purr braided through both, a thread of continuity that kept the night sewn up.

Marisol leaned back, the draft rising in her like breath after a held note. The pattern was not tidy enough to belong to her client, not messy enough to belong to chance. It felt like the beginning of a word.

Her phone buzzed again. She clicked it awake.

ISLEY: Bless you forever. How's it going?

She looked at the drawing of the bookstore that was supposed to be an office lobby and typed:

MARISOL: Rerouting in progress.

She almost added something absurd like Also mapping anomalous myth vacancies but decided against it. She set the phone down.

"Okay," she told the lines that were not supposed to be bookshelves. "Let's see what you want."

She reached for the compass. The motion was simple—thumb on the hinge, forefinger on the leg—and the metal in her hand remembered every circle she'd ever drawn. She set the needle in the center of the case seam and scribed a shallow arc, then another, then a full circle that crossed the empty marks in three places. Her breath shortened. She adjusted the radius, drew another. The arcs intersected with a gentle inevitability that made her spine tingle.

It wasn't a bullseye. It was a flower. A

rosette of whispered geometry. Any architect would call it pattern language. Any librarian would call it: someone is choosing.

Finn had moved without her noticing; now he sat at the nearer edge of the paper, green eyes wide, the tip of his tail stub tapping—a metronome set for decision. He leaned in, nose nearly touching the intersection where three arcs met.

"This?" she asked him. "Or that?"

He breathed on the paper—an invisible fog that she felt but did not see. She watched the leg of the compass shiver the smallest fraction, as if the table had exhaled.

"Don't be theatrical," she told it, which was a bit like telling rain not to be wet.

Her hands moved again, pencil now a needle stitching across the vellum. A hexagon emerged—one she hadn't planned and yet had planned all along. At each vertex: a missing book. At the center: the seam.

She sat back and let out a sound that could have been a laugh if it hadn't tripped over amazement on the way out. "You have a plan," she whispered, and didn't know whether she meant the bookstore or the thing inside it or the quiet intelligence of the space that held all three of them together— the shop, the cat, the woman with a pencil and an ordinary life that had begun to slant.

The radiator clicked an agreement. Or a

warning. They sound the same in apartments like this.

She stood and crossed to the kitchenette, boiled water she didn't strictly need, and came back with a mug she did. Finn rearranged himself on the drawing as if committing cartographic oversight. He pressed one paw exactly on the place where the circle crossed the seam, and he didn't move it when she returned.

"You're right," she said. "That's the hinge."

He blinked once, slowly and priestly, then pushed his head under her free hand with such force she almost dropped the tea. She set the mug down and obliged, rubbing the exact spot between his ears that made him rearrange himself into a puddle of good behavior.

"Let's name what's missing," she said softly, not to tempt fate so much as to cheat it. "Red canoe. Fox woodcut. Which one was the stag?" The words skittered away like minnows from a foot; her mouth knew the shapes and could not keep them. Her jaw went loose with the effort and then softened into resignation. "All right. Not yet."

She pulled another sheet, laid it on top of the map of Ink & Ivy that had hijacked an office plan, and began a clean overlay—just the rosette, just the hexagon, just the seam.

She drew the ivy wallpaper in schematic vines along the line where wood met plaster, not because she needed it for the map but because it was true. She wrote in the upper corner with tiny, precise letters: Ink & Ivy — central geometry (speculative). Underlined it once. Wrote the date. Drew a small cat in the margin because he was there and the world felt too delicate not to honor its ridiculousness.

Her phone buzzed again. This time it was her mother, who never texted this late unless she wanted to share a picture of a cloud that looked like a spoon or a quote from a book she hadn't quite enjoyed.

MOM: You up? Your uncle found the step stool. It was in the shed behind the rakes. How exciting. Also, I tried that recipe you sent—too much lemon. You would love it.

Marisol smiled. The normalcy of the message steadied her like a hand to the shoulder. She typed back:

MARISOL: I am up. Congratulations to the stool. Less lemon, noted. Love you.

She added a picture of Finn pretending to be the head of a small, powerful department and sent it. Three dots appeared, then:

MOM: Handsome boy. Tell him I said to behave. Love you more. Goodnight.

"Grandmother says don't eat the wallpaper," Marisol told Finn.

He pretended not to hear and placed his paw more firmly on the seam.

The night adjusted around the new drawing, as if furniture had shifted in a room behind a closed door. Marisol took a breath that looped through her like a ribbon. She sharpened the pencil, touched the point to the paper, and in the space that had never been a space, she drew a tiny symbol beside the seam—a circle with six petals. Not a sigil, she told herself. Just a mark you make when you want to remember the shape of a thought.

She looked at it too long and felt foolish and relieved at once. "Don't be dramatic," she told herself. "It's only lines."

Finn made a small, satisfied sound, as if he disagreed.

Before she rolled the overlay, she copied the rosette to a fresh scrap and slipped it into the little leather notebook she kept in her bag for measurements and grocery lists and phrases she liked: parsley, persistent; lintel; invisible cities; library fist (which had turned out to be a typo for "list," but she'd kept it anyway). She closed the notebook with a rubber band that had once held asparagus together and felt a ridiculous surge of competence.

The wall wasn't rerouted yet. The client would still have opinions. The missing books were still missing. But she had a shape now. She had a place to stand.

Finn yawned hugely, like a lion finishing a long aria, and then, in a motion she knew as well as her own heartbeat, padded along the edge of the table and pressed his nose to the very center of the rosette. For the briefest instant, the paper rose—no, not rose; that was silly—the paper seemed to breathe.

Her scalp prickled. She didn't touch the spot. She didn't move.

"Okay," she whispered. "Tomorrow, we test something."

Finn looked up, eyes wide as coins. He put a paw on the leather notebook. She laughed, startled, and felt the laughter open a window inside her chest.

"You'll come," she said. "Obviously."

He turned three circles on the corner of the vellum, folded himself back into his wry, convinced loaf, and closed his eyes. The purr returned, quiet now, a backbeat to the kind of silence that knows it is not alone.

Marisol switched off the task lamp. The apartment shifted from exacting work light to the forgiving amber of the floor lamp by the couch. She rinsed her mug in the tiny sink and dried it because she liked that ending even when there wasn't one. She washed the graphite from her fingertips, admiring the way it left a shadow in the whorls no soap could find. She turned back to her drafting table and, with care, slid the Ink & Ivy overlay under a clean sheet labeled CLIENT—LOBBY/ REV 3. The professional drawing went on top, because morning would come, and she would need to hand a world made of steel and codes and very stubborn walls to someone who did not believe in seams that hummed.

She lifted Finn from the corner to the couch, and he allowed it, performing a limp, boneless collapse that suggested she had saved his life. She turned off the lamp, and the apartment went blue with the kind of city darkness that remembers streetlights. Outside, a bus sighed and moved on.

"Goodnight, little kingdom," she said habitually, and realized, as she said it, that she meant both the one on the corner of her street and the one on her table. "Hold together."

Finn opened one eye, blinked deliberately, and closed it again.

She lay in bed with the window cracked and the blueprint of a bookstore on her mind. Between waking and sleep, her hands kept drawing circles. Between waking and sleep, the circles kept finding each other. Between waking and sleep, in the thin seam where night and morning shelve themselves side by side, she thought she felt the gentle hum in the bones of her wrist and the slightest lift of paper under a cat's paw.

When the dream finally took her, it smelled of paper and oranges and rain. And somewhere, like a page turning in a quiet room, a soft voice—not language but shape—whispered that a pattern had announced itself, and the shelves were listening back.

5 Finn Slips Through

The following evening, Ink & Ivy was already humming by the time Marisol slid the key into the lock. The bell above the door gave its usual bright chime, and the warm, papery air met her like a sigh of relief. She balanced her drafting tube under one arm, a grocery bag with two oranges in the other.

Finn trotted up from the back as though he had been waiting precisely for this moment. His whiskers twitched, his green eyes narrowed in mock disapproval, and he gave a short, sharp meow that sounded uncannily like *You're late.*

"Yes, Your Highness, traffic was atrocious," Marisol said, setting the oranges on the counter. "I'll try to reroute the interstate next time."

Finn sniffed the fruit, then batted one decisively off the counter so it rolled in an uneven circle across the rug. He pounced after it, his tail-less body executing an enthusiastic sideways hop that made Marisol laugh out loud.

"Fine," she said. "Exercise. I'll count that as your shift."

Customers drifted in as the rain started again outside. Addison appeared in a blur of sneakers and questions about dragons. Mr. Chartrand arrived with a cough of damp wool and a request for "something with teeth, but kinder teeth this time." Even Mrs. Marquel trundled in, umbrella dripping, demanding "a book that will tell me how to keep squirrels out of my compost without firearms."

The evening was filled with lamplight and the rustle of pages. Marisol poured tea, answered questions, stacked cookies on napkins, and watched the rhythms find themselves. All the while, Finn made his rounds, slipping between ankles and chairs, brushing his face against books as if anointing them.

It wasn't until the last customer had departed that the air shifted. The rain eased to a whisper on the glass, the shop's lamps glowed a little lower, and the hush after business hours settled in—a hush Marisol loved best. She turned to the shelves in Mythology, meaning to check on the dustless outlines she couldn't forget.

Finn got there first.

He trotted to the end of the aisle, his ears keenly forward. He leapt onto the bottom rung of the tall rolling ladder and from there onto the second shelf as though gravity had signed a truce. Marisol hurried over, hissing, "Finn, no—customers see claw marks, and I'll never hear the end of it—"

But Finn ignored her. He moved

deliberately, paw over paw, until he reached the shelf where the gaps had been. He pressed his nose against the seam between the two bookcases, whiskers trembling, then leaned his weight onto one spine: a dull green hardcover with no title.

The book shifted.

Marisol froze. She knew this shelf. She knew every spine, every dent, every title. And she knew that book had not been there yesterday.

Finn pressed harder. The spine swung inward, not like a falling book but like a hinge. The shelf creaked, a sound both wooden and not, and the air behind it gleamed faintly, as though lit from a place that shouldn't exist.

"Finn," Marisol whispered, pulse jumping.

The cat slipped forward, vanishing into the glow without hesitation. His whiskers were the last thing she saw before the shelf swung softly shut.

Marisol stood rooted, one hand braced on the ladder, the other on her pounding heart. She stared at the green spine—perfectly ordinary now, slotted among its neighbors.

"Did you just—" she began, and broke off, because she was speaking to a shelf.

She tugged the spine. It didn't budge.

She tried again, harder, but it held firm, heavy as if nailed in place. She pressed her palm to the seam. The wood felt warm.

"Finn?" she called softly. Her voice echoed in the empty shop, thin against the hush.

For a moment, just the barest slip of a moment, she thought she heard him: a faint, familiar trill, muffled, as though it came from a room behind the wall.

Then silence.

Marisol sat down hard on the rug, oranges rolling out of the grocery bag beside her. She picked one up, cradled it absently, and whispered into the golden hush, "If you come waltzing out of there on your own, I swear I'm installing a time clock."

But her voice shook, and her hand stayed on the seam as if it could will him back through.

Marisol sat cross-legged on the rug, one orange in her hand, the other wobbling against the leg of the ladder like a clock that had lost its sense of time. She kept her palm pressed to the seam, half afraid it would cool and half afraid it wouldn't.

Then, there. A faint vibration under her skin, followed by a muffled thud from the other side. The green spine jolted once, twice, then popped forward as though spat out. The shelf gave a reluctant sigh, wood groaning in complaint, and Finn tumbled back into the aisle in a flurry of fur and indignation.

He landed on his paws, shook himself once, and gave her a look that could only be translated as *What?*

Marisol let out a laugh that cracked in the middle. "You—Finn—you were—" She clutched the orange tighter. "Don't *do* that to me."

Finn stretched luxuriously, yawned wide enough to show the ridges of his palate, and then trotted straight to the counter. He leapt up, sat squarely by the register, and began washing one paw with a studied calmness that screamed innocence.

"You disappear into a glowing bookcase, and you come back acting like you've just woken from a nap." Marisol pushed herself to her feet, brushing dust from her skirt. "I should ground you. Can you even ground a cat?"

The bell above the door jingled before she could scold him further. Addison stuck her head in, cheeks flushed from the drizzle outside. "Forgot my backpack!" she called, darting between the shelves. She retrieved it from the armchair where she'd left it, then stopped when she noticed Marisol's expression. "Everything okay?"

"Fine," Marisol said too quickly. She

smoothed her hair with one hand. "Finn just gave me a scare."

Addison narrowed her eyes. "He *does* that. Once, he stared at the same corner for ten minutes straight. Nearly convinced me the shop was haunted."

Finn, still at the counter, paused mid-groom to look directly at her. He blinked, deliberate and slow, then resumed licking his paw.

"See?" Addison said. "Creepy." But she grinned as she swung her backpack onto her shoulders. "Bye, Miss. Callan. Bye, Finn. Try not to start a ghost uprising."

The bell chimed again as she left, her sneakers squeaking down the street.

The shop settled into its after-hours hush once more. Marisol righted the oranges, set them in a bowl behind the counter, and busied herself with closing tasks. She wound the clock, stacked a few stray returns, and straightened a display that rcfused to stay upright. Every few minutes, her gaze flicked to Finn, still on the counter like a carved guardian.

Finally, she carried the broom down the aisles. When she reached Mythology, she slowed. The dustless rectangles were still there—more of them now, she thought, though she couldn't swear to it. Her throat tightened.

She felt the urge to touch the seam again, to test it, to see if it would give. But Finn padded over, brushing against her ankles, purring with a force that nearly drowned out the silence. He butted his head against her shin until she bent down to scratch him. His green eyes gleamed, steady and anchoring, as if to say: not tonight.

"All right," she whispered. She leaned her forehead briefly against the oak shelf, then straightened.

By the time the last lamp was dimmed, the rain outside had softened to a mist. The shop glowed golden in the windows, a lantern on the cobbled street. Marisol slipped on her scarf, gathered her bag, and whispered the same words she always did: "Goodnight, little kingdom. Hold together."

Finn leapt to her shoulder with surprising lightness. His purr vibrated against her collarbone, a low, steady hum. Marisol chuckled, though her heart still beat a touch too fast. "Next time you vanish into the walls," she told him, "I'm docking your pay."

Finn butted her cheek with his head and purred louder, unconcerned.

She turned the key in the lock, and together they stepped into the damp night, the shelves behind them rustling in a language she wasn't quite ready to hear.

6 The First Visitor Returns

The next evening began gently, the way Marisol liked best. The rain had retreated, leaving the cobbles outside glazed like old ceramic. A calm wind nudged at the shop's sign, making the chain creak like a lullaby. Inside, Ink & Ivy stretched awake under her touch—lamps glowing, the kettle whispering, the shelves settling with their familiar wooden sighs.

Finn emerged from the poetry section with a smugness that suggested he'd been conducting inventory all day. He hopped onto the counter, curled himself directly across the stack of fresh receipts, and blinked at her with the kind of deliberate slowness that could disarm armies.

"You're not allowed to unionize without me," Marisol said, rubbing his head. He purred like a small, satisfied engine.

The bell chimed, letting in the smell of wet stone and the shuffle of Mr. Chartrand's coat. He paused in the doorway, glasses fogged. "Evening, Miss. Callan. And to His Majesty."

Finn chirruped, as if bestowing a blessing.

Not long after, Addie darted in, dripping enthusiasm and crumbs from the muffin she'd been eating on the run. "Do you have the second book in the series?" she asked before even dropping her backpack.

Marisol pulled it from under the counter with a magician's flourish. Addison squealed, snatched it, and sank into her armchair with Finn instantly abandoning the receipts to claim the armrest beside her.

The shop breathed into its rhythm—tea poured, chairs creaked, conversations curled through the aisles. It was all lamplight and page-turning until the bell over the door chimed again.

This time, the air shifted.

A tall man stepped inside, his coat too heavy for the mild evening, his smile too wide to belong to comfort. His skin was pale, not in the fragile way of an elder but in a way that made you think of paper left in the sun too long. He paused just inside the door, eyes sweeping the shelves not with curiosity but calculation.

"Good evening," Marisol said, her practiced warmth faltering by a thread.

The man's gaze landed on her, then on Finn, who was still perched by Addie. His lips curved. "I'm looking for a particular volume. *The Almanac of Autumn Winds.* You'll have it, surely."

Addison looked up from her chair. "Never heard of that one."

Marisol steadied herself. "I'm afraid it doesn't ring a bell. Could you be thinking of something else? *Seasonal Folklore,* perhaps?"

The man stepped further in. His shoes made no sound on the rug. "No. *The Almanac of Autumn Winds.* I read it once. Pages the color of rust. A chapter on orchards that bloom in smoke. Remarkable book." His eyes flicked toward the mythology section, then back to her. "It should be here."

Finn abandoned Addison's chair with a sudden, decisive leap. He padded across the shop floor and sprang onto the counter, tail stub twitching like a metronome wound too tight. He fixed the man with an unblinking stare, the kind of feline scrutiny that could unmake composure. Then, slowly, deliberately, he hissed.

The sound was low and long, vibrating through the shelves.

Mr. Chartrand froze mid-page. Addie's mouth dropped open. Marisol's pulse jumped in her throat. Finn seldom hissed.

The man's smile never faltered, but something sharp flickered behind it. "Ah," he said softly, "a discerning guardian." He inclined his head to Finn, not mockingly, but with an odd seriousness. "Well, keep your secrets, then."

He turned back toward the door, pausing only to brush his fingertips across a display of new releases. The gesture was so casual, but when he lifted his hand, the cover of one book seemed duller, as if the color had been pulled a shade away.

The bell chimed once as he stepped out. The street swallowed him whole.

Silence hung in his wake, heavy as a quilt.

Addison finally broke it. "That guy was weird. Who even asks for a book nobody's ever heard of?"

"Some collectors are eccentric," Marisol said, though her voice lacked conviction. She looked down at Finn. He still sat rigid on the counter, fur raised along his back, eyes fixed on the door as though he could see past it. His throat rumbled, not a hiss now, but a low, uneasy growl.

Mr. Chartrand cleared his throat. "You know," he said, "I do remember something about a book like that. Just a wisp of memory. An orchard, yes. But—" He shook his head firmly. "No. I must be misremembering. My age invents things."

Addison shuddered, pulling her backpack closer. "Whatever it was, I don't like him." She reached out, scratching Finn between the ears. He leaned into her hand but kept his eyes on the door.

Marisol forced herself to smile. "Well, thankfully, our ghosts are made of paper and ink. Nothing scarier than that." She busied herself with the kettle, pouring tea she didn't need, letting the steam blur the view of her own shaking hands.

But later, when the shop emptied and she dimmed the lamps one by one, she couldn't shake the feeling that the shelves were holding their breath. Finn followed her closely as she made her rounds, his green eyes catching the light in every corner. He leapt to her shoulder as she turned the lock, and when she whispered her ritual goodnight, "Goodnight, little kingdom. Hold together." His purr came out low, rough, and watchful, as though promising he would stand guard long after she slept.

Marisol spent the morning hunched over a drafting table at the firm, her pencil sliding across vellum in crisp, steady lines. The office hummed with fluorescent lights and the soft clatter of keyboards, her coworkers murmuring over deadlines and copy sets. Usually, she found comfort in the neat geometry of her work—the way a stubborn wall could be persuaded into harmony with a corridor, the way every line had a reason, a rule.

But today her hand trembled. Her eraser smudged more than it corrected. She caught herself shading not the stairwell she was meant to render, but a faint arch that looked suspiciously like the rolling ladder track in Ink & Ivy. The paper blurred, and suddenly she was back in the shop again, watching Finn vanish through the seam between the cases, the green spine swinging like a door hinge.

"Marisol?" Isley, her colleague, leaned over the divider. "You good? That's the third time you've drawn the north wall two feet too long."

She blinked down at the sheet, cheeks warming. "Sorry. Long night."

Isley gave her a knowing grin. "You need more sleep or more coffee. Maybe both." He dropped a paperclip onto her desk like a peace offering. "Take a break before you redraw the entire lobby sideways."

She forced a smile. "I'll grab tea."

But when she went to the break room and filled her mug, she found herself sketching absentmindedly on a napkin: the outline of the missing books, the soft curve of a shelf that wasn't supposed to bend. She crumpled it quickly, heart thudding.

By the time she walked back through the cobbled streets toward Ink & Ivy that evening, her thoughts were still knotted. She carried her drafting tube under her arm, but it felt heavier than its weight.

The bell above the shop door chimed its warm, familiar note. Relief washed through her shoulders. The smell of old paper and cinnamon grounded her in a way office air never could.

Finn trotted forward immediately, tail stub twitching with annoyance, as if scolding her for leaving him with managerial duties all day. He leapt onto the counter, gave a stern meow, and began pawing at her drafting tube.

"You want to see the blueprints?" she asked, amused despite herself. "They're not nearly as interesting as disappearing shelves."

Finn batted the tube again, then sat on it, declaring victory. His whiskers twitched smugly.

"Fine," Marisol sighed. "But if you spill tea on client work, I'm blaming you."

Customers drifted in. Addison, bright-eyed and eager, dropped her backpack on the armchair and launched into a recap of her book's dragon duel. Mr. Chartrand arrived slower, muttering about moss and the cruelty of daylight savings. The baker stopped by with a paper bag of still-warm rolls "in case anyone needed fortifying."

The shop filled with its evening rhythm. Marisol poured tea, handed out bookmarks, and listened to the pages turn. Yet her mind kept circling back to the seam. She caught herself staring at it more than once, her hand tightening around the teapot whenever Finn prowled too close.

And then, as if on cue, Finn slipped away from his admirers. One moment, he was curled on Addie's armchair, the next, he was scaling the ladder with feline determination. Marisol set down a tray of cups too hard, heart clenching.

"Finn," she whispered, striding toward him.

He pressed his nose against the green spine. It shifted with that same impossible hinge. Before Marisol could stop him, he pushed through. A faint glow spilled out, haloing his whiskers, and then he was gone.

The shelf swung shut as if nothing had happened.

Marisol stood frozen, tea cooling in her hands. Addie's chatter and Mr. Chartrand's quiet murmurs blurred into background noise. All she could hear was her pulse and the silence that followed Finn's disappearance.

Minutes stretched. Her throat tightened. Then, with a sudden thud, the green spine popped back. Finn tumbled out, fur slightly puffed, eyes wide. He shook himself once, then padded toward her as though nothing unusual had occurred.

"Where—" Marisol choked on the question. She crouched, scooping him into her arms. "Don't do that! You can't just—"

Finn purred loudly, pressing his face against her chin, and flicked his ear dismissively as if to say *all in a day's work.*

Addison glanced up. "What's wrong?"

Marisol forced her voice steady. "Nothing. Just...he was climbing where he shouldn't."

"Finn climbing where he shouldn't?" Mr. Chartrand said dryly, adjusting his glasses. "Perish the thought."

The laughter that followed was warm, and the evening folded back into its cozy pattern. But when the last lamp was dimmed and the door locked, Marisol carried Finn to the counter, holding him close against her chest. His purr thrummed deep, steady as a heartbeat.

"Whatever that was," she whispered, "you're not doing it again without me."

Finn blinked slowly, then tucked his head beneath her chin, the picture of innocence. His fur smelled faintly of something she couldn't place—like leaves turned in autumn wind.

7 Dust & Memory

The morning began with fog—thick and low, curling across the cobblestones like a cat reluctant to leave its bed. Marisol pedaled her bike through it, scarf pulled high, eyes still haunted from dreams she couldn't quite pin down. Something about shelves that leaned into endless corridors, Finn's green eyes glowing like lanterns, her pencil sketching circles that refused to stay flat.

By the time she pushed open the door of Ink & Ivy, the fog had followed her inside, clinging to the windows in soft halos. The bell chimed its polite greeting. Finn was already perched on the counter, paws tucked beneath him, as though he had been waiting all along. His gaze was calm, steady, too knowing for an animal whose morning should have consisted of breakfast and naps.

"You didn't wait up all night for me, did you?" Marisol asked, setting down her satchel.

Finn blinked slowly, then yawned so wide his whole face became teeth and pink tongue. He leapt down, padded to the rug, and stretched with the long, indulgent grace of someone whose schedule was entirely self-made.

Marisol flicked on the lamps one by one, watching the shop's corners bloom into amber warmth. She filled the kettle, straightened the displays, and let herself ease into the rhythm that had become ritual. But even as she dusted the front table, her eyes kept straying to the seam in the mythology section.

She told herself she wouldn't touch it. Not yet. Not until she understood what Finn had done.

Instead, she drifted to the back where the large, oversized atlases lived—big, leather-bound beasts that took both arms to carry, relics from when books had been built to outlast buildings. She had been meaning to reorganize them, though few customers ever ventured this far. The fogged window lent the aisle a cathedral hush.

She tugged at a particularly weighty volume, its spine cracked but still proud. *Atlas of the Known and Forgotten Worlds,* the gilt lettering read. Dust rained down in lazy spirals as she eased it free. She carried it to the counter, Finn following with an unusual intensity, his tail-stub flicking in short, sharp beats.

"Don't look at me like that," she told him. "Even librarians need exercise."

She laid the atlas flat, its leather cool under her palms. The cover gave off the faint, dry smell of cedar. When she opened it, the pages sighed like lungs remembering breath. Maps sprawled across each spread—oceans inked in faded blues, mountains raised in delicate hatch marks, cities marked with stars that seemed almost to twinkle under lamplight.

Finn hopped onto the counter, settling beside the atlas. He bent his head, sniffed, then pawed delicately at the margin of one page as if trying to draw her attention.

"What are you—"

Her words caught.

There, tucked between two maps, was a folded sheet of paper, browned at the edges. Not a publisher's insert, not the stiff kind of library slip. This was something older, softer, and more fragile than parchment. Marisol's pulse jumped as she slid it free.

Finn's eyes locked on the paper. His whiskers trembled.

She unfolded it with care, expecting an old receipt or a bookseller's note. Instead, her breath stopped.

The handwriting was unmistakably her own.

Her name in her own hand stopped her breath halfway up her throat.

Marisol. If you're reading this, you haven't yet decided what to give up.

The pen strokes were so familiar—her careful loop on the *r*, the way she pressed harder on downstrokes as if conviction were a physical thing. She touched the ink with the pad of her ring finger; it was long dry. Years? Days? The letters sat on the page with the confidence of something that had been waiting.

Finn leaned close enough that his whiskers grazed the margin. He made a soft *mmrp* and settled, tail-stub ticking like a small clock.

Marisol swallowed, then read on.

You will think you imagined the gaps. You will tell yourself your eyes were tired and you mis-shelved a book, perhaps two. You will want to believe that because it is easier to hold a wrong book than a vanishing. Don't go gently into the explanation that hurts least. The shelves are speaking. You already know it—your bones knew before your head did.

She paused. The kettle on the hot plate began its tiny, anticipatory whisper. She ignored it. The shop's early light lay in quiet squares across the counter; the atlas's maps looked like sleeping creatures.

You have found the seam. Good. Don't pry. It isn't a door, the way a door is a door. Doors forgive. Seams remember.

Finn's head snapped up at the line, as if he recognized a tune he loved. He blinked at her, slow and solemn. She glanced down, almost expecting to find his pawprint in the margin beside the sentence, as if he'd signed off on the advice.

You want rules. You are a drafter. Here are the ones you can bear:

1. Every third.
2. Hexagon at the heart.
3. A circle closes what a hand can't.
4. The shop will take a tithe, but you may choose the currency.
5. You will not do this alone.

Her mouth went dry. She reread the list, heart climbing the staircase of her ribs, one careful tread at a time. Every third. Hexagon at the heart. She saw last night's overlay—the rosette, the six points where the missing books aligned, the compass's legs drawing arcs that knew more than she did.

"Did I write this?" she whispered.

Finn head-butted her wrist, a small, decisive *yes* that only muddied things further.

She forced her gaze down again, to the next paragraph, written with a firmer hand. The line of a woman trying not to shake:

They will ask for *The Almanac of Autumn Winds.* It is not a test you can pass by refusal. The man who wants it is not a customer; do not give him a customer's grace. He is tidy, and tidiness is not the same as care. He believes stories can be made efficient by subtraction. He will call them redundancies, and you will think of your neatest plans, your most elegant solutions. Don't let the rhyme trick you. We are not solving. We are holding.

She felt again the strange flattening of color when the pale man's fingers grazed a cover. The wrongness that had slunk into the room in his wake. Finn's hiss, unheard in years, stretches the silence taut.

"Okay," she breathed. "Okay."

The kettle clicked itself off, ignored. Dust glittered, slow as snowfall, in the wedge of light by the register.

You will be tempted to bargain with the shelves. (And with yourself. Especially with yourself.) You will offer labor in place of loss. You will offer sleeplessness and precision and the good manners of your hands. The shelves don't want your manners. They want the truth. When the price comes due, pay it with a memory you can spare but will miss. Choose what you give. If you don't choose, the seam will.

Her skin pebbled. Something in her—stubborn, practical—rose in protest like a hand in a meeting: *I have nothing to spare.* But another part—the one that had stood before the seam and felt it hum under her palm—knew the shape of a tithe when it heard one.

"What would we even—" she began, then couldn't finish the sentence aloud. Finn's ear rotated toward her, his body warm where it leaned against her forearm.

There was a blot where the ink had pooled, as if the writer had lifted the pen to think and the pen had thought on its own. Then:

When you doubt (you will), look to the pattern, not the panic. Lay your lines. Overlay the shop. Let the compass make the case that your mouth can't. Draw circles until the fear has to sit down and rest. Then move the circle one degree. If the arc touches the empty places in rhythm, you are still in step with the story.

Marisol let out a sound that was not quite a laugh. "That's exactly what I did," she said, more to her hands than to the room.

Finn reached—delicately, inexcusably— and set one paw on the letter as if to keep it from blowing away in a wind that did not exist. His claws stayed sheathed. His weight was enough to say *this matters*.

The letter's last third came denser, words pushing against each other as if the writer had been warned the page would soon run out.

You will want names. (Red canoe. Fox woodcut. A stag etched so fine you can feel the burr of the line.) Names will slither. That's part of the taking: not just books, but the language of them. Don't tug on the loose end. Hold the shape. Keep a ledger of outlines if you must—draw the space a book leaves and label that. It helps.

She thought of the tiny rectangles she'd sketched as placeholders on the shelf last night, drawn because she felt foolish and somehow less so for admitting it with a pencil. She hadn't meant to be obedient to a letter she hadn't yet found. And yet.

There is a woman in the orchard in *The Almanac.* She is older than she looks and younger than she sounds. Suppose you meet her (and you will, if Finn behaves like Finn), do not tell her your whole name. Do not tell her what you are willing to pay. Ask her instead where the wind goes in winter. She will laugh and say, "Sideways." Ask her where stories go when they are stolen. She will stop laughing. Listen. She is the Keeper. She will not call herself that.

Marisol's mouth formed the word without sound: Keeper. It felt the way oak feels when you run your hand along the grain that wants to be stroked in one direction only.

And then, more gently, almost tender despite the tightness of the letters:

You love the straight rule of things—the *click* when the triangle sits flush, the ribbon of graphite when the line is true. Keep that. You will need it. The shop chose you for your eye and your stubborn heart and the way you say "Goodnight, little kingdom. Hold together." (It hears you.) Let your hands do what they know. Draw the ritual on the floor when the time comes. Ink, a compass, and the stones from the lake you pocketed last summer. Finn will sit where he should. You will know which corner to round and which to keep sharp.

She pressed her lips together; her eyes stung suddenly and unreasonably. She hadn't told anyone about the stones. Three smooth ovals from the lake's edge. Paperweights. Anchors. A private superstition that felt like childhood without being about childhood at all.

The last lines were smaller, as if the writer had run out of room and refused to run out of saying:

When it is worst, remember: we keep so the keeping keeps us. We guard because we were guarded. The seam is a seam because two things meet there that would rather be whole. You are not alone. (Look down. He's there.)

Marisol did. Finn, having judged his work complete, had slid into a loaf so exact he could have been drawn with a French curve. He lifted his face and met her gaze, green bright as sea glass, then butted her wrist, once, as if to seal a pact.

There was a postscript, squeezed along the outer margin in that awkward sideways way she'd used for grocery lists when she'd run out of paper:

P.S. If you are reading this on a morning with fog, be brave by afternoon. The fog is kind. It makes the street quiet enough to hear the shelves listen back.

The kettle had cooled. She hadn't noticed when it stopped whispering. In the quiet, the letter seemed to hum with the rest of the shop, as if it were more a tool than a message—something you could hold up to the light to check alignment.

Her hands shook only a little as she refolded the page along its original creases. The paper remembered the fold the way a muscle remembers a dance. She slid it into the atlas again, then hesitated. Her chest tightened at the thought of leaving it there, hidden, away from her skin.

Finn solved it by reaching out, catching the corner between his teeth, and tugging. Gently, absurdly, he began to drag the letter toward the edge of the counter like a kitten relocating a toy mouse.

"Hey," she said, half laughing, half warning. "Careful."

He released it and looked pointedly at her bag.

"So we're not leaving this for someone else to find," she translated, and folded the letter smaller. She slipped it into the leather notebook—measurements, grocery lists, phrases—and banded it shut with the tired asparagus rubber. The notebook felt heavier immediately, as if a different kind of math lived in it now.

Behind her, the bell over the door gave a small, testing jingle, like a throat clearing before speech. She looked up, startled, but no one stood there. The fog at the windows lifted a fraction, letting in a little more day.

She closed the atlas gently and stroked the scarred leather of its cover as if to thank it for holding. Then she carried it back to its place on the bottom shelf, lifting with her legs the way the mover in her head always reminded her to. Finn trotted at her heel like a dog in a book about a farm where everyone knows where the eggs are kept.

"Every third," she murmured, mostly to the pattern buzzing at the edges of her vision. "Hexagon at the heart. A circle closes what a hand can't. A tithe. Not alone."

Finn rubbed his face against the seam as they passed, and the oak warmed beneath her palm again, polite and certain. She didn't press. Not yet. The letter had asked her not to be brave by morning. She had until the afternoon.

She returned to the counter, poured water that was too cool to deserve the name tea, and drank it anyway because endings matter. She set the mug down carefully and, because the letter had said looking down would help, she did. Finn stared up at her, pupils wide as coins, tail-stub tapping twice, then still.

"Okay," she told him, and the shelves, and the piece of herself that had written to the piece that was still pretending to be surprised. "We'll draw circles."

The bell chimed for real this time. The day began to arrive—wet coats, questions, familiar faces haloed in fog. Marisol slid the notebook into her bag, patted it once like a promise, and turned toward the door with a bookseller's smile and a drafter's plan behind her eyes.

Finn leapt to the counter, sat with all the dignity of a paperweight carved from living velvet, and began to purr—a low, steady sound that stitched the morning to whatever would come next.

By late morning, the fog outside had thinned enough to reveal a handful of pedestrians braving the damp cobblestones. Ink & Ivy glowed like a lantern, its windows haloed in condensation. The first to push through the door was Mr. Chartrand, shaking droplets from his umbrella with the air of a man wringing sense from stubborn weather.

"Miss. Callan," he said warmly, then tipped his head toward the counter. "Your Majesty."

Finn, already seated in prime position on the atlas Marisol had not quite managed to put away, blinked slowly, receiving the homage.

"Careful," Marisol said, hurriedly shifting the book beneath the counter. Her hands lingered too long on the leather, as if unwilling to let it go. "How are you this morning, Mr. Chartrand?"

"Still vertical," he replied, eyes twinkling. "And still hungry for something with teeth." He rubbed his gloved hands together as though sharpening them.

"Teeth we have," Marisol said, fetching a slim collection of Sylvia Plath's journals from Poetry. She placed it into his hands with a flourish.

"Ah." He cradled it with reverence, as if the book itself were breathing. "Perfect."

The bell jingled again, this time announcing Addison, who tumbled in with a backpack half-zipped and a grin that could have lit the fog on its own.

"You *will not* believe what happened in chapter twelve," she blurted before her coat was even off. She collapsed into her chair and pulled her book from the bag like a magician producing a dove. "Dragons *and* librarians. Can you imagine?"

"Obviously," Marisol said, fighting a smile.

"Obviously," Addison agreed, already thumbing back to the page.

Finn abandoned his guard post on the counter and trotted over to Addison, hopping into her lap with the casual entitlement of someone certain he was the main character. She laughed, scratching his chin until his purr grew so loud it practically joined the kettle in harmony.

Marisol busied herself with the ritual of tea, the motions grounding her: mug, bag, water, steam. She moved among her customers, answering questions, recommending books, and tidying displays. To anyone looking, she was the picture of ease, her smile warm, her voice calm.

But beneath the surface, her mind kept circling the folded sheet now tucked deep in her notebook. The neatness of the handwriting, the shape of the words, the rules it laid out like blueprints. Her own hand had written it, somehow. And though she hadn't told anyone, she kept feeling as though the shelves knew.

The bell jingled a third time. The baker arrived, a paper bag balanced on one arm.

"Thought you might need fortification," he said, setting it on the counter. "Cinnamon knots this morning."

Finn materialized instantly, nose twitching. He sat at the baker's feet and meowed so plaintively it could have melted stone.

"You," the baker said, crouching down, "are shameless." He tore a corner of bread and placed it gently on the floor.

Finn sniffed once, ate it neatly, then sat back with regal satisfaction.

"Don't let him fool you," Marisol said, sliding the bag open and inhaling deeply. "He had breakfast already."

"I don't doubt it," the baker said, eyes fond.

The chatter rose and curled around the shelves, pages turning like soft applause, laughter weaving in small, bright threads. Ink & Ivy felt alive with its own quiet joy.

And yet—Marisol's gaze kept flicking toward the back of the shop, where the atlases slept. Every so often, she thought she heard a faint rustle there, like paper sliding against paper without a hand. Finn would lift his head, ears angling, before resettling himself in Addison's lap as if nothing were amiss.

Still, she felt it: the shop listening back.

By the time the afternoon light slanted across the rug in golden bars, the shop had grown quiet again. Mr. Chartrand had wandered out with his journals tucked beneath one arm, Addison had dashed off to meet a friend with promises to report back about dragons, and the baker had left the cinnamon knots but carried away a mystery novel in exchange.

Marisol relished the hush. She locked the register drawer, poured herself the last inch of lukewarm tea, and leaned against the counter. For a moment, she almost believed she could return to ordinary things: invoices, shelving, the draft she owed Isley by morning.

But her bag sat on the stool beneath the counter, and in it was her notebook. And inside that—the letter. Her own handwriting where no memory lived.

She pulled it out halfway, then froze. What would happen if she read it again? Would the words shift? Would they accuse her of cowardice? She shoved the notebook back into her bag, biting her lip.

Finn, who had been lounging by the atlas shelves, suddenly leapt down. His paws barely whispered against the floor as he padded toward her. He sniffed her bag once, then with surprising delicacy, slipped his teeth into the corner of the notebook and tugged.

"Don't you dare," Marisol warned, crouching.

He tugged again, harder this time, dragging the notebook an inch out of the bag. Then he looked up at her, green eyes bright with challenge, and gave a chirrup that sounded like *Well?*

"Finn…" She ran a hand over her face. "You're relentless."

He batted the notebook with one paw, sending it tumbling onto the rug. The rubber band slipped, the pages splaying open just enough for the folded sheet to show. Finn sat beside it, tail-stub flicking, as if waiting for her to admit what he already knew: ignoring it wouldn't make it vanish.

Marisol sank onto the rug, legs folding awkwardly beneath her. She picked up the paper, smoothing the creases with her palm. The ink looked no different than it had that morning, but the words seemed to breathe against her skin. She could almost feel the pressure of her own pen in the downstrokes, the echo of her hand across time.

"Do I tell someone?" she whispered. "Do I show Addison? Mr. Chartrand? Would they even believe me?"

Finn tilted his head, blinked once.

"It's absurd," Marisol muttered. "Who finds a letter in their own handwriting predicting things that already happened? I should throw it in the fireplace and be done."

The cat's gaze sharpened, ears angling back ever so slightly. He gave a low, throaty sound—not hostile, but insistent.

"All right," she sighed. "Not the fireplace." She folded the sheet smaller, tighter, and slid it back into the notebook. "But I can't keep this to myself forever."

She thought of Addison, so bright and earnest, too young for strange burdens. Mr. Chartrand, steady but aging, carrying his own quiet weight. The baker, the regulars, her coworkers at the firm—ordinary people with ordinary days. None of them deserved to be tangled in whatever Ink & Ivy had hidden in its seams.

And yet, the letter had said *you will not do this alone.*

Her stomach knotted. Alone was her preference. Alone was tidy. Alone was safer for everyone else. But Finn nudged her hand with his head, purring as if to remind her that alone wasn't on the table anymore.

She pressed her forehead briefly against his fur, closing her eyes. His warmth seeped into her like an anchor.

"Not tonight," she whispered. "Tomorrow I'll decide who to trust."

The bell over the door chimed then, startling her upright. A pair of customers stepped in, dripping with evening drizzle, their chatter brisk and harmless. Marisol forced a smile, tucking the notebook beneath the counter once more.

Finn remained on the rug, watching, his tail-stub tapping like a metronome—an unspoken reminder that secrets, once uncovered, never stay quiet for long.

By evening, the drizzle outside had thickened into a fine mist that blurred the streetlamps into hazy halos. Ink & Ivy held itself warmly against the damp, its lamps glowing like pockets of sun. A few late customers trickled in—an office worker in need of something "not spreadsheets," a pair of teenagers looking for ghost stories, Mrs. Marquel with her endless war against squirrels.

Marisol greeted them all with the same steady warmth, but her mind kept tugging at the folded sheet in her notebook. The letter's words seemed to echo in the cadence of conversation, surfacing in strange places: *Every third... A circle closes what a hand can't... You will not do this alone.*

Finn made the rounds, brushing against ankles, tolerating pats, and finally returning to his station on the counter. Each time her gaze strayed toward the back shelves, his eyes followed, green and unblinking.

By closing, the fog had crept right up to the shop's glass, blurring even the nearest lamppost. The last customers trickled out, the bell chiming softly after them. Marisol flipped the sign to CLOSED, locked the door, and leaned her forehead briefly against the cool pane.

The hush after hours pressed into a hush she usually loved. Tonight, it was thick with listening.

She turned back to the counter. Her bag lay open, the notebook peeking out. She pulled it free, opened to the middle where the letter waited, and hesitated.

"Not tonight," she whispered, echoing her promise to Finn earlier. Carefully, she refolded the sheet, slid it back between the notebook's pages, and stretched the tired asparagus rubber band across the cover. She tucked the notebook into the deepest pocket of her drafting tube, a hiding place that felt almost ceremonial.

The shop exhaled. At least, that's how it sounded—the faint rustle of shelves settling, a susurration of paper. Marisol froze, hand on the counter. The noise didn't belong to the old pipes or the kettle cooling on the hot plate. It was quieter than that, like pages turning where no hand rested.

Finn's ears went forward. He rose onto his haunches, tail-stub twitching, and gave a short, decisive chirp. Then he leapt to the floor and trotted to the mythology section.

Marisol followed, heart tight. The seam between the cases looked ordinary in the amber lamplight. The green spine sat firmly in place. But the air around it seemed thicker, as if the fog had seeped through the walls.

"Not tonight," she told the shelves. Her voice shook but didn't falter. "You'll keep."

Finn circled her ankles once, then pressed against her shin, a solid presence anchoring her to the moment.

She dimmed the lamps one by one, the shop shrinking into pools of gold, then ember, then soft shadow. At the door, she whispered her nightly benediction: "Goodnight, little kingdom. Hold together."

Finn leapt to her shoulder, purring low, the sound vibrating against her collarbone. Outside, the fog wrapped them close, muffling the world into softness. The cobbles gleamed under the blurred light, as if the whole town had slipped into a dream.

And behind them, just as she turned the key in the lock, a single page rustled.

Marisol slept with the window cracked, the fog pressing close like a second curtain. Finn curled at her feet, heavy and warm, his purr ebbing into silence as he slipped into his own depths.

Her sleep began the way it often did—faces from the day reshuffled, streets familiar yet skewed. But soon the dream sharpened, taking on the clarity of ink on vellum.

She stood in an orchard. Rows upon rows of trees stretched outward, their branches not laden with fruit but with pages—thin, fluttering sheets that rustled in the night breeze. Each page was handwritten in a different script: some spidery and small, some bold and blocky, some in languages she couldn't name. When the wind stirred, the branches whispered, and the orchard sounded like a library trying not to wake someone.

Her shoes sank slightly in soil the color of old leather. The air smelled faintly of smoke and apples at once, though no apples hung on the boughs. She reached out to touch a page. It was soft, weathered. The ink was fading, but she could just make out words: *the canoe red as blood, paddled by no one, gliding across the lake at dawn.*

She snatched her hand back. She *knew* that story. She had shelved it once, perhaps twice. But she could not call its name.

"Sideways," said a voice.

Marisol turned.

At the far edge of the orchard, where the trees bent as if curtsying to one another, stood a woman. Her hair was the gray of ash, but her face seemed neither young nor old—rather, she looked assembled from many ages, as if the years had refused to settle on just one. She wore a coat the color of fallen leaves and carried no lantern, yet the pages glowed faintly around her as she passed.

"You're the Keeper," Marisol whispered, remembering the letter's words.

The woman's mouth curled into a smile, not unkind but unreadable. "That isn't what I call myself." Her voice sounded like paper rubbed between fingers—dry, delicate, and strong enough to cut.

"Where...where does the wind go in winter?" Marisol asked quickly, clumsy with urgency.

The woman laughed, the sound bright and unsettling. "Sideways."

The orchard rustled in agreement, branches bending in the strange current of a wind Marisol could not feel.

"And where do stories go when they are stolen?" Marisol pressed, her throat tight.

The Keeper's smile fell away. She looked directly at Marisol, eyes glinting like wet ink. For a moment, silence swallowed even the whisper of pages. Then she said softly, "Nowhere you would want to follow."

Something shifted then. The trees closest to Marisol bowed inward, their branches knitting together above her. The pages brushed her hair, her shoulders. They whispered—not words, not quite—but syllables that felt familiar, like the hum of the seam behind the mythology shelf.

Finn appeared at her feet. In the dream, he was the same and not the same: his body glowed faintly at the edges, like a figure drawn over in silver pencil. He sat square, tail-stub flicking, and looked up at her with absolute certainty.

The Keeper tilted her head toward him. "Not alone," she said. "You see? He already knows the price."

Marisol bent down, scooping Finn into her arms, though in the dream he felt both weightless and impossibly heavy, as if he were made of every stone she'd ever pocketed. "What price?" she asked, voice breaking.

The Keeper didn't answer. She only stepped backward into the trees. Pages curled and shivered in her wake, falling like leaves into the soil. The orchard dimmed, the words slipping away, until Marisol was left standing in silence.

She tried to follow, but her feet rooted to the soil. She looked down and realized the ground beneath her was no longer soil at all but a quilt of empty book-shaped outlines, their spaces neatly drawn, waiting to be filled.

When she woke, her cheeks were damp.

The window was still cracked. The fog pressed in, silver with dawn. And Finn, curled at her feet, lifted his head to look at her with wide, unblinking eyes—as if he, too, had seen the orchard.

Morning broke reluctantly, the fog still sprawled across the streets like a quilt that hadn't been folded. Marisol sat at her drafting table, hair unbrushed, mug of tea cooling beside her. She had rolled a fresh sheet of vellum across the oak surface, pinned at the corners by her three lake stones and one heavy book—*Collected Myths of the Midwest,* borrowed from her own shelves.

The letter's rules echoed in her mind: *Every third. Hexagon at the heart. A circle closes what a hand can't.*

She sharpened her pencil, the familiar rasp soothing, and drew a single straight line to steady herself. It was meant to be the outline of a lobby wall for the project Isley had begged her to reroute, but her hand wavered. The line tilted into the shape of a shelf.

Finn leapt onto the table without apology. He inspected the stones, shoved his nose into the pencil cup, then flopped directly across the lower edge of the vellum. His purr vibrated through the paper, a soft bassline to her hesitation.

"You're supposed to be my assistant," Marisol said, nudging him. "Not quality control."

Finn blinked, slow and imperious, and stretched his paw across the sheet until it landed squarely in the space she'd just drawn. The graphite smudged under his pads, leaving faint ghost-marks shaped like pawprints.

Marisol laughed despite herself. "Fine. Co-author, then."

She reached for her compass, adjusted the hinge until the legs spread wide, and pressed the point into the vellum. The circle unfurled beneath her hand, arcs meeting arcs until the shape grew into a flower again, petals touching where the gaps should have been.

Her chest tightened. The pattern was the same as before, only clearer now. A geometry not of walls or rooms but of absences.

She moved the compass one degree, as the letter had suggested. The arc shifted, and suddenly every missing point aligned in rhythm, like notes on a staff. She felt it before she understood it: a vibration through her wrist, a quiet hum that echoed the seam in the shop.

Finn's ears pricked. He rose onto his haunches, paw tapping the center of the circle. He gave a short, insistent *mrrp*.

"You see it too," Marisol whispered.

The compass wobbled in her hand, metal trembling as if the table had a pulse. She set it down quickly, heart pounding. The circle lay innocent on the vellum, but she couldn't shake the sense that it was listening.

Finn sat, tail-stub flicking like punctuation, eyes fixed on her face.

"All right," she murmured, sliding her hands over the drawing as though to calm it. "I believe you. I believe us."

She folded the sheet carefully, slipped it into her notebook beside the letter, and closed the cover. The asparagus rubber band strained to hold the weight of both.

When she looked up, the fog at the window had thinned just enough to show the outline of Ink & Ivy's sign swinging gently in the breeze, as if reminding her where the real work waited.

Finn settled into a loaf at the edge of the table, content, his purr resuming like a motor put back into gear.

Marisol sipped her cold tea, gaze steady on the circle she could still see in her mind. For the first time since the gaps appeared, she felt less like she was losing something and more like she had been invited to draw the blueprint of a secret that wanted keeping.

"Good," she told Finn, and herself, and the quiet hum she could almost hear. "Then we'll keep it."

8 The Pale Man Returns

The day after the orchard dream dawned sharper, the fog thinned into pale morning light that left the cobblestones damp and shining. Marisol pedaled to the shop, the drafting tube bumping against her back. She had tucked the notebook—with the letter and the circled vellum—deep inside. The weight of it felt heavier than paper should, as if she were carrying a secret blueprint in her bones.

Ink & Ivy greeted her as always: the bell chimed, the ivy wallpaper glowed in the angled light, and the shelves gave their settling sigh. Finn appeared from the poetry section, stretching in a long arc before trotting up to her shoulder height. He chirruped softly, then leapt onto the counter, watching her with the same bright scrutiny he'd given the compass circle.

"Good morning to you, too," she said, stroking his head. "Still keeping the kingdom in line?"

He blinked in dignified confirmation.

The morning unfolded in its usual cozy cadence. Mrs. Marquel arrived first, bearing more squirrel complaints and leaving with a book on companion planting. Addison rushed in next, eyes sparkling, desperate to share a passage about dragon librarians. The baker followed, balancing a tray of rolls dusted in sugar. Soon the shop was filled with laughter, the rustle of pages, and the gentle fog of kettle steam.

Marisol breathed easier, carried along by the rhythm of her little kingdom. For a few hours, she almost convinced herself the letter had been nothing more than an imaginative trick, a stress-born invention of her overworked brain.

Until the bell chimed.

The pale man stepped inside.

His coat was heavy despite the mild weather, his shoes silent on the rug. His presence drained warmth from the room as surely as an open window in winter. Customers fell quiet, their voices dimming as if someone had lowered a curtain.

"Good day," he said smoothly, his smile practiced but thin. His eyes swept the room before finding Marisol. "I thought I might try again. Perhaps you've come across it since last we spoke—*The Almanac of Autumn Winds*?"

Marisol's throat closed. The letter's warning flared bright in her mind: *He believes stories can be made efficient by subtraction.*

"I'm afraid not," she said carefully. "We don't have it."

Before the man could reply, Finn leapt from the counter to the floor, a streak of gray fur and muscle. He planted himself between Marisol and the stranger, tail-stub twitching in staccato bursts. His fur rose along his spine, and a sound rolled from his throat—not the hiss from before, but a deep, steady growl that vibrated through the floorboards.

The pale man paused, studying him. "An impressive guardian," he murmured. He crouched slightly, extending two fingers in mock invitation. "Come, then."

Finn did not move. His eyes narrowed, pupils thin as ink slits. His growl deepened.

"Finn," Marisol said softly, her hand trembling at her side.

The man straightened, his smile sharpening. "Well," he said. "Perhaps another time. Books have a way of surfacing when they are ready." His gaze lingered on the mythology section. "And some books have a way of vanishing when they shouldn't."

The air seemed to hold its breath.

Then he tipped his hat, turned, and left. The bell chimed once, and the street swallowed him whole.

For a long moment, silence reigned. Then Addison let out a shaky laugh. "What was *that* guy's problem? He's like...an accountant crossed with a vampire."

Mr. Chartrand adjusted his spectacles; his expression clouded. "I almost remember the title he asked for," he said softly. "Almost. But it slips."

Marisol busied herself with the kettle, hiding the tremor in her hands. "Collectors can be...eccentric," she said, though the words tasted false.

Finn padded back to her side, pressing against her shin with deliberate weight. He purred once, loud, defiant, before hopping back onto the counter and sitting squarely as if declaring the kingdom safe again.

The chatter slowly returned, but the rhythm felt off-kilter, like a clock that had lost half a beat. Even as she smiled and served tea, Marisol felt the weight of the letter in her bag, humming in time with Finn's purr.

When the last customer left that evening and the shop's hush returned, she whispered her benediction at the door: "Goodnight, little kingdom. Hold together."

And in the quiet, the seam in the mythology section seemed to hum back.

The last lamplight of the evening pooled gold across the rugs. Marisol moved slowly through her closing rituals—checking the register, stacking stray books, washing mugs one by one. She found comfort in the small order of it, though her hands lingered too long on each task.

She paused at the back of the shop, adjusting a crooked bookend in Gardening. That's when she heard it again: the faint hum, low and insistent, rising from the mythology section. It was like the sound of bees buried deep in a wall, easy to ignore if you weren't listening, impossible to forget once you were.

Marisol's throat tightened. She turned toward the seam.

The green spine sat innocently in its row, but the space around it seemed thicker, the air pressing in on itself. A draft tickled her ankles, though the window was shut.

"Not tonight," she whispered, though her voice lacked conviction.

Finn padded up beside her, silent as a thought. His ears pricked forward, his whiskers quivering. He leapt lightly onto the ladder rung and from there to the second shelf, until his nose nearly brushed the seam. He sniffed once, then looked over his shoulder at her, eyes bright as lantern glass.

"Don't you start," she said, reaching up to scoop him down. But before she could, the shelf gave a faint click, like a latch loosening. The green spine shivered.

Marisol's heart lurched. She pulled Finn into her arms, holding him tight against her chest. His body vibrated with a low, urgent purr—not fearful, not warning, but steady, as though he were trying to remind her that she wasn't alone.

The hum faded. The shelf stilled.

Marisol stood in the aisle, her heartbeat loud enough to drown the silence. She pressed her forehead briefly to the top of Finn's head. His fur smelled faintly of dust and cinnamon rolls.

"All right," she whispered. "Tomorrow."

Back at the counter, she brewed herself a fresh mug of chamomile, though she didn't truly want tea. She opened her drafting tube and pulled free her notebook, laying it on the table beside the steaming cup. The asparagus rubber band stretched tight, guarding the folded letter and her circled vellum.

She stared at the cover. Her hand hovered, wanting to open it, wanting to trace the arcs again, to feel the pattern steady her. But the pale man's face rose in her mind— his too-wide smile, his strange attention to the shelves. The thought of him seeing her drawings made her stomach knot.

Finn jumped up onto the counter, planting himself directly on top of the notebook. He turned in a tight circle before loafing neatly, his eyes closing as if to say *No one gets through without me.*

Marisol let out a shaky laugh. "Good. You're hired."

She pushed the mug toward him. He sniffed the steam, made a face, and turned his head with great dignity.

For a long time, she sat with him like that—the cat a warm, steady weight on her secrets, the tea cooling beside her, the shelves rustling faintly like a house settling after a storm.

When she finally dimmed the lamps and went to lock the front, she heard it: the faintest stir of wind at the door, though the fog outside lay heavy and still. It curled beneath the crack, cool against her ankles, carrying the dry scent of paper.

Finn jumped down from the counter and padded to the door. He sat squarely before it, tail-stub twitching, his gaze fixed on the seam of light between door and floor. He didn't hiss. He didn't growl. He simply watched.

Marisol knelt beside him, her hand resting on his back. Together, they waited as the wind whispered once more, then faded.

She turned the lock, her hand trembling. "Goodnight, little kingdom," she whispered, the words more plea than benediction. "Hold together."

The shelves answered with a soft rustle, a single page turning somewhere in the dark.

Finn pressed against her calf, then padded back to the counter. His purr rose again, quiet but steady, as if sewing the sound of the shop closed for the night.

Marisol slept lightly, the fog pressing close to her window like a hand against glass. Finn curled above her head on the pillow, his purr a low, steady tide that usually carried her into safe harbors.

But her dreams carried her elsewhere.

She stood again in Ink & Ivy, only it was hollow, stripped of warmth. The lamps were unlit, the air thin, the rugs bleached to gray. The shelves stretched higher than the ceiling, their ladders vanishing into shadow.

The pale man walked the aisles with careful precision, his shoes making no sound. One by one, he touched the spines of books, and with each touch, a title vanished. A shelf that had been full shrank into neat gaps—gaps in rhythm, every third book gone. He moved without hurry, as though subtraction were the most natural thing in the world.

Marisol tried to speak, but no words left her throat. Her hand lifted, wanting to stop him, but when she reached for a book, her fingers closed on nothing but air.

The man turned, his smile thin, his eyes pale as unwritten paper. "Efficiency," he said softly. "Stories should not wander. They should march."

And with a sweep of his hand, an entire row disappeared—no dust, no spines, only absence arranged neatly in their place. The shelves groaned under the subtraction, wood bending not with weight but with want.

Marisol's chest ached. She wanted to cry out that stories weren't columns of figures to be balanced, weren't walls to be squared—but her voice stayed trapped.

Only then did Finn appear, leaping onto the counter in the dream-shop. He opened his mouth wide and hissed, the sound reverberating so loudly the pale man faltered. The hiss filled the aisles like a storm, rattling every shelf. Pages tumbled from nowhere, fluttering down like leaves in autumn.

The pale man's smile slipped. For the first time, his eyes narrowed. He lifted one vanished hand—smooth, blank, uncreased by use—and reached toward Finn.

Marisol woke with a gasp, her heart pounding, hand clutching the bedsheet.

The room was dark, but Finn was there, pressed warm against her shoulder, his eyes open, watching the door. His purr rolled steady, louder than usual, as if stitching her back into the waking world.

Outside, the fog moved against the glass like the turning of a page.

9 Ledger of Outlines

Marisol arrived at Ink & Ivy earlier than usual, bike tires hissing across damp cobbles. Dawn was pale, the fog already retreating, leaving the windows streaked with dew. She unlocked the shop with a hand that still trembled faintly from the night before. The dream clung to her: the pale man subtracting shelves, Finn's hiss rattling the aisles.

The bell chimed its bright, ordinary note. The shop breathed back into life—lamps glowing, rugs holding the scent of cinnamon and old wood. She exhaled, relieved to find everything exactly as she had left it.

Except not exactly.

The mythology section had two new gaps. Small, precise, too neat to be an accident.

Marisol's chest tightened. She walked straight to the shelves, notebook in hand. She slid the asparagus rubber band off with care, opened to a fresh page, and drew two new rectangles—outlines of absence. She labeled them only with a question mark, just as she had before.

Finn padded up, leapt onto the nearest shelf, and sat squarely in the middle of the gaps. He pressed his paws into the wood as if staking a claim, then looked down at her, eyes bright.

"Guarding the missing?" Marisol asked softly. "Or keeping count?"

Finn blinked once, slow, deliberate. Then he tapped the shelf twice with one paw.

"Ledger, then," she murmured. She flipped back through her notebook. Six missing. Now eight. The pattern is growing like geometry.

The bell chimed behind her. She startled, quickly closing the notebook and tucking it under her arm.

"Morning, Miss. Callan!" Addison burst in, hair frizzy from the damp, backpack bouncing. "I brought muffins!"

The word *muffins* summoned Finn instantly. He hopped down from his guard post and trotted toward her, tail-stub twitching like a metronome of anticipation. Addison laughed, setting the paper bag on the counter. "I swear he knows that word."

"More likely he knows *you*," Marisol said, amused despite her nerves. She fetched plates, grateful for the distraction.

Soon, Mr. Chartrand arrived too, settling into his favorite corner with a book of elegies. The baker followed, carrying extra rolls "for trading purposes." The shop filled with warm chatter, the kettle humming its companion song.

Marisol poured tea, handed out muffins, and smiled at the familiar rhythm. And yet—her gaze kept straying to the seam, to the ledger of absences in her notebook, to the memory of the pale man's hand brushing away titles like crumbs.

She excused herself between customers and returned to the counter, sliding the notebook open beneath the till. The outlines stared back at her, eight blank shapes, a pattern not yet finished. She traced the latest two with her pencil, her hand steady despite her racing thoughts.

Finn hopped onto the counter, sprawling across the open page. He purred loudly, as though to drown out the silence of the gaps. Then, with one paw, he dragged her pencil across the paper. The graphite line cut diagonally, linking two of the empty outlines.

Marisol froze.

"That's not random, is it?" she whispered.

Finn purred louder, tail-stub flicking once.

Her throat tightened. She drew another line, connecting the next absence. Then another. The pattern emerged slowly, as if the shelves themselves were sketching through her hand: a hexagon's skeleton, unfinished but undeniable.

She sat back, breath catching.

The bell chimed again, letting in the cool damp of afternoon—and with it, a flicker of unease. Marisol closed the notebook quickly, pressing her palm to the cover as if to hold the pattern in place.

Finn stayed on the counter, watching the door. His ears twitched once, sharp, before he curled neatly into a loaf, tail-stub tucked, as if pretending nothing at all had happened.

But his eyes never left the seam.

The day stretched on, steady as rain on a roof. Addison tucked herself into her usual chair, a muffin in one hand and a fantasy epic in the other. Mr. Chartrand scribbled notes in his margin with the concentration of a scholar. The baker lingered by Gardening, pretending to browse while dropping crumbs on the rug.

Marisol tried to busy herself with invoices, yet her gaze kept darting toward the seam. She could feel it even when she didn't look—like a low hum in her chest, a pressure that pulled her attention.

"Miss. Callan?" Addie's voice carried from her chair.

Marisol startled. "Yes?"

Addie squinted down the mythology aisle. "Weren't there more books here? I swear, last week there was a green one about, uh, wolves or something."

Marisol's heart lurched. She forced a calm smile. "Shelving shuffle. Sometimes I move sections around."

"Really?" Addison frowned. "I don't remember seeing you do it."

Mr. Chartrand looked up from his notebook. His spectacles slid down his nose. "I recall that one, too. Cover with a wolf in profile. Strange, isn't it? I can picture it, but not the title."

Marisol's pulse quickened. "I'll check the backroom. It may have been misfiled." She fled toward the storeroom before they could ask more.

Inside, she pressed her palm to her eyes. You can't keep lying forever, the letter's words whispered back.

Finn slipped in behind her, tail-stub flicking. He sat on the storeroom floor, gazing at her with sharp patience. His whiskers trembled as if he, too, heard the shelves murmuring.

"You're right," she whispered to him. "But not yet."

When the shop quieted again, Marisol opened her notebook at the counter. She sketched the wolf's outline from memory— jaws, spine, tail—and filled the blank rectangle with it. Another absence, another mark.

Finn hopped onto the page, paws pressing graphite shadows into the vellum. He pawed at her pencil until she let him bat it, then nudged it back toward her with surprising precision.

"All right," she murmured, adding a line where he had placed it. "Co-authored again."

The hexagon sharpened. Eight gaps now. The geometry is growing.

Finn purred, eyes half-closed, but his body remained taut, ready, like a guard pretending to nap.

As dusk painted the windows, the bell jingled again. A stranger stepped inside: a man in a rain-slick coat, ordinary enough. He asked for directions, browsed quickly, bought a travel guide, and left.

Yet the moment he brushed past mythology, Marisol thought she saw the green spine quiver. Just a flicker, but enough to clench her stomach.

Finn hissed—quiet, brief, but unmistakable.

The shop fell silent. Even Addison looked up, wide-eyed. "He's never hissed at *me*," she whispered, half in awe.

Marisol forced a laugh, her throat dry. "He's a good judge of character."

Finn hopped down and pressed against her leg, his fur hot.

At closing, Marisol stacked mugs, turned out lamps, and whispered her benediction: "Goodnight, little kingdom. Hold together."

The seam hummed faintly, like a page turned by invisible hands.

She carried Finn upstairs to her small flat above the shop, where she often stayed when nights ran late. He sprawled across her drafting table, batting idly at her compass while she tucked her notebook into the drawer.

"You won't let me keep secrets, will you?" she asked softly.

Finn looked up, pupils wide, then stretched his paw across the circle she had drawn the night before. The graphite smeared faintly under his pads.

"Co-authored," she murmured again, brushing her hand over his fur.

He purred, deep and low, until the shelves below seemed to hum with him. Marisol closed her eyes, the sound wrapping around her like a promise: she wasn't alone. Not anymore.

10 Confidences

Morning light pooled through the shop windows in long rectangles, dust motes drifting like quiet constellations. Marisol unlocked the door, flicked the lamps on, and set the kettle to hum. She felt stretched thin, as if she'd left part of herself in the orchard dream and part on the vellum circles upstairs. Her bag was heavier than ever, the notebook pressing insistently against her hip.

Finn followed her like a shadow, trotting to the counter before vaulting onto it with his usual ease. He sat squarely in the middle of the day's receipts, tail-stub tapping, green eyes fixed on her face.

"I know," she murmured, scratching his chin. "I can't keep this to myself forever."

The bell jingled, and in swept Addison—bright as a firecracker, hair damp from drizzle. She dropped her backpack with a thud and grinned. "Guess what? My mom says I can help out here officially on weekends. Like, with the till and everything. Isn't that amazing?"

Finn chirruped, leaping straight into her arms as though to approve the appointment. Addison laughed, spinning once in the entryway with him clutched against her.

Marisol smiled, warmth tugging at her lips despite the knot in her stomach. "That's wonderful, Addison." She hesitated, then added: "I...could use your help."

Addison tilted her head, surprised. "With what?"

Marisol's throat tightened. She wanted to spill everything—the gaps, the letter, the ledger of outlines. But the memory of the pale man's too-smooth smile stopped her. Addison was young, bright, and unguarded. Was it fair to hand her a piece of this weight?

"Reshelving," Marisol said finally, forcing a smile. "There've been...odd gaps lately. Books misplaced. I'd like you to keep an eye out."

Addison's eyes narrowed. "You mean, like, books disappearing?"

Marisol laughed too quickly. "Nothing that dramatic. Just poor filing."

But Addison wasn't convinced. She glanced toward mythology, chewing her lip. "Funny. Mr. Chartrand said he thought he saw a book there yesterday that wasn't there today."

Marisol froze.

The bell chimed again, and Mr. Chartrand himself entered, humming under his breath. He carried his worn satchel, from which a corner of his notes poked out. "Morning, ladies," he greeted warmly. He stopped at the counter, glanced at Marisol, and lowered his voice. "Strange thing—I could swear I'm misplacing my own memory. That wolf book? It isn't just gone from the shelf. It's gone from my head. I know I read it. I can picture the ink on the page. But I cannot, for the life of me, recall a single sentence."

Marisol's breath caught.

Finn growled—a low, rolling sound—then hopped down from Addison's arm and stalked straight to mythology, planting himself before the seam as if to underline Chartrand's words.

"See?" Addison whispered, her voice hushed with awe. "Finn knows."

Mr. Chartrand adjusted his spectacles, his eyes gentle but sharp. "My dear, you look pale. Perhaps it's time you told us what you've been carrying."

Marisol's lips parted, the words trembling on her tongue. She could tell them. She could show them the ledger, the letter, the circle on vellum. She could admit that the shelves weren't simply losing books; they were swallowing them whole.

But just then, the kettle clicked. The sharp sound startled her, cutting the moment in two. She reached for mugs, hands shaking. "Tea first," she said, too quickly. "We'll talk with tea."

Behind her, the seam hummed.

Marisol's hand lingered on the mugs longer than it should have. Porcelain rattled faintly against porcelain. Behind her, Addison and Mr. Chartrand exchanged a glance—the kind adults share when they sense something hovering in the air but can't quite name it.

Finn sat before the mythology section, tail-stub ticking. His green eyes gleamed in the lamplight, fixed on Marisol as if daring her to go on.

"Here we are," she said too brightly, setting steaming mugs on the counter. "Chamomile for Addison, black for Mr. Chartrand." Her own hand trembled slightly as she poured hers.

"Thank you," Mr. Chartrand said, though his gaze didn't leave her face.

"Thanks!" Addison said, tearing into a muffin.

Marisol blew across the surface of her tea. The steam rose in delicate swirls, but it carried no comfort today. She could almost hear the letter whispering from her notebook: *You will not do this alone.*

Her voice snagged in her throat. "I...need to tell you something."

Both Addison and Mr. Chartrand looked up, expectant.

But before she could begin, the bell jingled and Mrs. Marquel bustled in, umbrella dripping, cheeks flushed. "Don't mind me," she called, bustling to Gardening. "Just after marigold lore today. Carry on!"

The moment was shattered. Marisol pressed her lips shut, tea scalding on her tongue.

When Mrs. Marquel disappeared into the aisles, Finn sprang into action. He leapt onto the counter, scattering receipts, then nosed straight into Marisol's bag. With surprising determination, he hooked the strap with his teeth and tugged.

"Finn!" Marisol hissed, trying to pull the bag back. But he was quicker, digging one paw inside and dragging out the notebook. It thudded onto the counter, rubber band stretched taut.

Addison's eyes widened. "Is that—?"

Before Marisol could snatch it, Finn stepped on the cover, tail flicking, and pawed the rubber band loose. The notebook spilled open, pages fluttering. And there, in plain view, were the empty rectangles she'd drawn: the ledger of absences.

Mr. Chartrand leaned closer, adjusting his spectacles. His breath caught. "Good heavens. You've been keeping record."

Marisol's face burned. She pressed her palms to the counter, struggling for words. "It's not—it's nothing. Just sketches. Notes."

But Finn gave a loud, scolding *mrrrow*, stamping his paw directly on the latest outline.

Addison leaned forward, eyes wide with awe rather than fear. "Those are the books, aren't they? The missing ones."

Marisol swallowed hard. Her secrets lay bare under the cat's paw.

The shop felt too still, as though every shelf strained to hear. The seam hummed faintly in the background, a low vibration that threaded the silence.

Marisol forced herself to speak. "They're not just misplaced. They're...gone. Vanished."

"Vanished?" Addison whispered.

"Yes." Her voice cracked. "And it isn't just the books. It's our memories of them, too. Titles, passages, whole stories. Like they were never here at all."

Mr. Chartrand's face grew grave. He reached out, touching the notebook gently, as though steadying her. "I knew it. I thought it was my own mind faltering. But it's the shop, isn't it? Or something inside it."

Marisol nodded, breath trembling. "I found a letter in my handwriting. It warned me about this. About a man looking for *The Almanac of Autumn Winds*."

Addison gasped. "The pale guy. The one Finn hissed at."

At the sound of his name unspoken, Finn growled again, a rumble that vibrated through the counter.

Marisol pressed her hand over the notebook, trying to keep her courage steady. "I don't understand it. But I can't keep pretending it's normal."

Mr. Chartrand sipped his tea, thoughtfully. "Then you've done the right thing. Secrets rot in silence. Better shared."

Addison reached out, resting her hand briefly over Marisol's. "You're not alone. You have us. And Finn, obviously."

Finn purred loudly, stamping her notebook once more as if sealing the pact.

The seam hummed louder. Books shivered faintly on the mythology shelf. The sound was so subtle it could have been dismissed as settling wood—except every person in the room turned toward it at once.

Mrs. Marquel reappeared from Gardening, obliviously, humming about marigolds. But at the counter, the three of them held their breath.

"Did it just—?" Addison whispered.

"Yes," Marisol said, her voice steady at last. "It hears us."

Finn's gaze never left the seam. His tail-stub tapped once, twice, then stilled. His body was poised as though ready to leap between worlds.

Marisol closed the notebook carefully, slid the rubber band back into place, and tucked it against her chest. "Then we keep the ledger," she said softly. "Together."

Mr. Chartrand inclined his head. Addison squeezed her hand.

Finn purred once more, low and certain.

And from the mythology shelf, a single page turned.

The seam hummed louder. Books shivered faintly on the mythology shelf. The sound was so subtle it could have been dismissed as settling wood, except every person in the room turned toward it at once.

Mrs. Marquel reappeared from Gardening, obliviously, humming about marigolds. But at the counter, the three of them held their breath.

"Did it just—?" Addison whispered.

"Yes," Marisol said, her voice steady at last. "It hears us."

Finn's gaze never left the seam. His tail-stub tapped once, twice, then stilled. His body was poised as though ready to leap between worlds.

Marisol closed the notebook carefully, slid the rubber band back into place, and tucked it against her chest. "Then we keep the ledger," she said softly. "Together."

Mr. Chartrand inclined his head. Addison squeezed her hand.

Finn purred once more, low and certain.

And from the mythology shelf, a single page turned.

11 Circles and Ledgers

The shop felt different the next morning, as though the very air had been listening to their conversation the day before. Marisol lingered with the key in the lock, Finn perched on her shoulder like a furry gargoyle, tail-stub ticking against her collarbone.

Inside, everything was ordinary—lamps warm, rugs welcoming, the faint scent of cinnamon lingering from yesterday's muffins. And yet: the shelves seemed watchful. Expectant.

Mr. Chartrand was already waiting with his satchel, spectacles perched low on his nose. He had brought a thermos of strong coffee, which he poured into paper cups with the solemnity of a priest sharing communion. Addison arrived minutes later, hair tangled from rain, clutching a folder of her own scribbled notes.

They gathered at the counter, mugs steaming between them. Finn sat squarely atop Marisol's notebook, paws folded neatly as if presiding over the meeting.

"So," Mr. Chartrand began, his voice low but steady. "We agreed not to let this fester in silence. The question is—what can we *do*?"

Marisol opened the notebook. The ledger's rectangles stared up at them, eight neat absences now half-bound by graphite lines forming a crooked hexagon.

"We track them," she said. "Properly. Not just sketches. A real ledger."

Addison grinned, pulling open her folder. "Already started." Inside were her hand-drawn grids, each space labeled with subject headings and shelf numbers. "I thought maybe we could cross-check every day. Like attendance for books."

Marisol blinked, impressed. "Brilliant."

Finn chirruped, nudging the edge of the folder with his nose.

"Then it's settled," Mr. Chartrand said. "We watch. We record. And when the pattern grows clearer, we decide what to do next."

They split up; each was assigned an aisle. Addison bounced toward fantasy, muttering titles under her breath as she checked them off against her sheet. Mr. Chartrand took history, his finger tracing spines like rosary beads.

Marisol moved straight to mythology. Her pulse quickened as she drew near the seam. The green spine sat still, but the air shimmered faintly—like heat over asphalt.

She crouched, notebook open, pencil poised. Two more gaps. Titles she half-remembered but could not name. She drew their outlines carefully, pressing harder on the pencil until the paper dented.

Finn padded up behind her and leapt onto the shelf itself, tucking his paws beneath him as though declaring ownership. His body vibrated with a low purr.

"Stay there," she whispered. "Keep watch."

He blinked slowly, solemn, as though promising he would.

By the time they regrouped at the counter, Addison's grid showed three absences in fantasy, one in history, and two in folklore. Marisol added her own. The ledger grew heavier with each mark, the hexagon sharper.

"It's accelerating," Mr. Chartrand murmured. "At this rate, entire sections will vanish."

Marisol pressed her hand to the page. "Not if we keep them tethered."

That evening, when the shop had closed, and Mrs. Marquel had gone off humming with her marigold book, Marisol brought out her drafting tools. She spread vellum across the counter, anchoring it with her three lake stones.

"The letter said a circle could close what a hand can't," she explained. "Maybe if we map the pattern onto the floor, it'll hold the books in place."

Addison's eyes lit. "Like chalk lines in fairy tales."

Mr. Chartrand nodded. "Containment."

Marisol set her compass, drew the first arc. The circle curved across the vellum, perfect and clean. She shifted one degree, drew again. Another arc, and another, until the lines overlapped in a rosette.

Finn hopped down, inspecting the vellum. Then he sat directly in the circle's center, tail-stub twitching. His purr rose until it filled the room.

The shelves rustled. Faint, but unmistakable. A whisper of pages, as though acknowledging the attempt.

"Did you hear that?" Addison breathed.

"Yes," Marisol said, her heart racing. She pressed her palm to the vellum. The arcs vibrated faintly under her hand, as though the lines themselves were alive.

For a moment, the gaps in her notebook seemed to steady, their shapes holding rather than slipping further.

Then the kettle clicked off, the spell of sound breaking. The rosette lay flat again, graphite on paper. The ledger pages fluttered once in a draft.

Marisol exhaled. "It's something. Not enough yet. But something."

They tidied the counter together, folding vellum, stacking notebooks, and pouring the last of the coffee into mugs. Mr. Chartrand lingered by the door, resting one hand on the shelf as though giving it a blessing. Addison gathered her notes with the seriousness of a knight entrusted with a quest.

When they were gone, Marisol locked the door and stood in the hush. Finn leapt onto her shoulder again, rubbing his face against her hair.

"Not alone," she whispered. "Never again."

The seam hummed faintly in reply. And for the first time, the sound felt less like a warning and more like an agreement.

Upstairs in her flat, Marisol rolled fresh vellum across the drafting table. The lamplight caught on the steel of her compass, the edges of her triangle, the tiny chips in her mechanical pencil. She breathed in the familiar scent of graphite and tracing paper, letting the ritual calm her.

She had deadlines, after all. Isley wanted revisions on the lobby plans by Friday, and here she was, tracing circles that weren't part of any building.

Still, her hands moved with automatic precision: walls measured to the millimeter, doors angled for smooth egress, staircases spiraling true. The work should have anchored her. But each clean line seemed to ripple, reminding her of arcs she had drawn downstairs on the counter—the rosette that had trembled under her palm.

She pressed harder, the lead snapping. She sighed, reached for another pencil. Her fingers brushed her notebook instead, lying at the edge of the table. Its rubber band bulged over the ledger of absences.

Finn leapt silently onto the table, his paws scattering erasers. He lay across the plans, his eyes half-lidded, purr a steady undercurrent.

"Not a drafting cat," Marisol muttered, shifting him gently.

He stretched anyway, a paw landing squarely on her half-finished lobby sketch. Right on the atrium. The spot she'd struggled with.

Marisol blinked. Where his paw pressed, her mind filled with the memory of the seam humming. *A circle closes what a hand can't.* She reached for her compass, hesitated, then drew an arc through the atrium. The curve caught the lobby's flow in a way her straight edges hadn't, easing the tension she'd been fighting for hours.

She sat back, startled. "That...works."

Finn purred louder, tail-stub flicking.

Her chest tightened. Drafting had always been about control, precision, things flush and square. But tonight, her lines curved, rosettes nested into blueprints, circles overlaying walls. And the more she let them slip into her work, the more the room seemed to listen.

The lamp's halo flickered. Her tea rippled as though someone had sighed across the surface. The ivy wallpaper rustled faintly, though no window was open.

Ink & Ivy was seeping into her plans. Or perhaps her plans were seeping into Ink & Ivy.

Marisol dropped her pencil, suddenly aware of how thin the distance was between shop and blueprint, between the ledger's hexagon and the walls she drew.

Finn settled on the notebook now, curling his body around it like a lock. His purr steadied, softer, almost coaxing.

"All right," Marisol whispered. She set her compass down, extinguished the lamp, and let the plans lie half-finished. "Tomorrow."

She crawled into bed with her mind full of circles, rosettes, and shelves humming in the dark. The kingdom below slept, or pretended to, but she dreamed again of walls bending toward books, and books bending back toward her.

That night, sleep came only in fragments. Marisol drifted in and out, the fog outside her window rising and falling with her breath. Finn curled at the crook of her knees, warm and steady, his purr a pulse against the silence.

Her dream began in the drafting office. The fluorescent hum above her was too bright, her desk littered with rolls of plans, coffee rings smudging the corners. Isley leaned over her shoulder, tapping the atrium with his pen. "Needs more efficiency. Straighter lines. Cut the curve."

She bent over the vellum, her hand obediently redrawing walls, sharper, thinner, stripping the flow from the space. But every time she pressed the pencil down, the lines bent back into arcs, blossoming into circles, then into rosettes. The paper trembled beneath her hand as if the drawing wanted something she couldn't give.

When she looked up, the office walls had melted into shelves. Endless rows of spines stretched upward, their ladders vanishing into shadow. Isley was gone. In his place, the pale man walked the aisles, his fingers brushing spines that vanished with every touch.

"No," Marisol whispered, but the word skidded across the floor like a loose pencil.

She tried to chase him, but her feet tangled in rolled blueprints that had unspooled across the aisles. The blueprints fluttered open on their own, revealing rosettes instead of walls, circles nested in circles, each arc connecting to the missing rectangles from her ledger.

The pale man stopped at the seam. He turned, smile thin as parchment. "Straight lines only," he said. "Order without waste." His hand reached toward the green spine—

And Finn appeared, launching from the vellum like ink splashed across the page. He landed on the seam with a hiss so fierce it rattled the ladders. Pages tore free from unseen books, swirling through the air like startled birds.

The man recoiled, narrowing his eyes. "He can't keep them forever."

Marisol reached forward, pressing her palm against the floor. The blueprints lit from beneath, the rosettes glowing like constellations. The shelves trembled, humming louder, joining Finn's hiss with their own defiant chorus.

She woke with a gasp, sweat damp on her collarbone. The room was still, her lamp dark. Finn sat on her chest now, his face inches from hers, eyes wide and unblinking as though he'd been watching her dream from the inside.

"Not forever," she whispered to him. "But maybe long enough."

Finn purred once, soft and deliberate, before curling back into sleep.

12 The Circle Holds

Ink & Ivy was never truly silent at night. Even when the lamps were dimmed and the door locked, there was always the soft creak of timber, the occasional thump of a book resettling in its sleep. But this night was different.

The vellum rosette lay spread across the counter, left where Marisol had abandoned it. Moonlight slipped through the window and fell directly across its arcs. The graphite shimmered faintly, as though the moon were ink and the lines thirsty.

The pattern seemed to be exhaling.

One by one, the gaps in the mythology section stilled. The hum in the seam softened, like a note resolving into harmony. The empty spaces felt less raw, less jagged— as if the circle had wrapped around them, holding them in place.

On the counter, Finn sat alert. He had not slept since Marisol drifted off upstairs. His body was still, but his eyes glowed in the dimness, fixed on the rosette. Each time a page whispered in the aisles, his ears flicked, but he did not move. Guardian at his post.

The circle held.

Just before sunrise, the ivy wallpaper rustled. Its leaves seemed to shift in a breeze that didn't exist, edges trembling as if alive. A page fell loose from one of the folklore volumes—not torn, not dropped, but released. It fluttered gently, landing in the center of the rosette.

The vellum drank it in. The page sank flat, no longer separate, as if the drawing had claimed it. Words faded, leaving only faint imprints in graphite arcs.

Finn meowed softly, once. Not alarm, but acknowledgment. He circled the counter, then curled directly against the edge of the vellum. His body pressed the lines in place, his purr rumbling like mortar sealing bricks.

When the morning light spilled through the fog, the shop looked ordinary again. Rugs soft, shelves full, the seam as still as oak. But the rosette remained faintly luminous under the new day, graphite lines sharper than when Marisol had drawn them.

And the missing books? Their outlines still lived in her notebook, but the ache of their absence had dulled. Not gone—but contained.

Marisol descended the stairs with heavy steps, rubbing sleep from her eyes. The smell of tea leaves drifted from the kettle, though she hadn't filled it.

Her gaze fell on the counter. The rosette glowed faintly in the morning light. At its center lay Finn, curled like punctuation, his body completing the circle.

She froze, heart lurching. "Did it...work?" she whispered.

Finn blinked at her, slow and sure.

She approached cautiously, fingers grazing the vellum. The arcs vibrated faintly, like a plucked string. The seam in mythology was quiet, its hum barely perceptible.

Marisol pressed her palm flat on the vellum. A calm warmth spread through her hand, traveling up her arm, easing the knot that had lodged in her chest for weeks. The letter had been correct: a circle could close what a hand could not.

She laughed softly, shaky with relief. "It held."

Finn rose, stretching luxuriously, then placed one paw firmly on her wrist. His eyes glowed with a knowing that unsettled and comforted her all at once.

"Not alone," she murmured, echoing the letter.

The bell over the door jingled just then, though she hadn't unlocked it yet. She turned, startled, to see Addison peering through the glass, grinning and waving a bag of croissants. Behind her, Mr. Chartrand raised a hand in greeting.

The day was beginning. The kingdom would wake. And for now, at least, the circle held.

The bell chimed again as Marisol hurried to unlock the door. Addison bustled in, a paper bag of croissants nearly as big as her backpack. "Fuel," she announced, cheeks pink from the chill outside.

Mr. Chartrand followed, nodding solemnly as though he too had carried something sacred. In his hands was a small, battered notebook bound with twine. "Comparative notes," he explained. "What I remember versus what I no longer do."

Marisol ushered them to the counter, her heart pounding. The rosette still lay across it, vellum glowing faintly where the morning sun touched it. Finn remained stationed on top, purr low, eyes bright as though he'd been waiting for an audience.

Addison froze mid-step. "Whoa." She set the croissants down carefully, as though any sudden movement might disturb the air. "Did you draw that?"

Marisol nodded. "Last night. The letter said a circle could close what a hand can't. I think...it worked. At least for now."

Mr. Chartrand leaned closer, his spectacles fogging slightly. "Remarkable. It radiates as if it were inked in light, not graphite." He extended a cautious hand, but

Finn gave a sharp *chirrup* and pressed his paw firmly on the vellum.

"Permission first," Addison translated solemnly.

Chartrand inclined his head toward Finn. "My apologies, sir."

Finn blinked slowly, then stepped aside, tail-stub flicking once as though granting limited access.

Mr. Chartrand placed his twine-bound notebook beside the rosette. "Let us see," he murmured, flipping it open. His neat handwriting filled the page: *Wolf of the Northern Pines. Author's name lost. Plot slipping.*

He tapped the words. "This is the book I could recall in outline but not in substance. Perhaps the circle will..." He trailed off, not daring to finish the hope aloud.

Addison leaned in, her eyes wide. "Try reading it inside the circle."

Chartrand hesitated, then slid the notebook across the vellum. The moment it crossed one of the arcs, the graphite lines shimmered faintly. Finn purred louder, tail vibrating.

The words on the page deepened, their faded edges sharpening as though ink had seeped back into them. Chartrand gasped softly. "I...remember the scent of pine resin. A boy chasing something through the snow." He looked up, tears glinting at the corners of his eyes. "I hadn't realized how much I'd lost until it returned."

Marisol pressed a hand to her mouth, overwhelmed. The circle was not only holding gaps in place—it was tethering their memories too.

Addison clapped her hands. "It's working! We've made, like, a magical book corral!"

Finn trotted a neat circle around the vellum, then flopped in the center again, tail curled tight. His purr filled the shop, steady as a heartbeat.

As if stirred by their discovery, the mythology section rustled faintly. A book slid half an inch outward, then back, like someone had tested its spine.

Addison jumped. "Did it just—"

"Yes," Marisol whispered. She walked to the seam, pressing her palm against the oak. It was warm, alive under her touch. "It knows."

The hum was there again, but different, less like a warning, more like a sigh of relief.

Mr. Chartrand closed his notebook carefully, his voice hushed with reverence. "We've given the shop a frame. And in return, it seems willing to let us keep remembering."

Marisol drew back, trembling with relief and fear at once. "Then we'll keep the circle here. Always."

Finn sneezed once, then gave a proud *mrrrow,* as though claiming the rosette as his invention all along.

The day passed in a haze of croissants, cautious laughter, and hushed awe. Customers came and went, oblivious to the shimmer at the counter, while the three of them took turns slipping notebooks across the rosette, testing half-remembered fragments. Some returned whole, others sharpened like a photograph brought into focus.

When dusk arrived and the last visitor left, Marisol dimmed the lamps. She lingered by the counter, fingertips brushing the vellum arcs.

"Goodnight, little kingdom," she whispered. "Hold together."

The circle glowed faintly, and the seam hummed in agreement.

Finn curled at the center of the rosette once more, his purr so deep it seemed to seep into the wood, into the shelves, into the stories themselves.

Marisol closed her eyes, a smile breaking through her exhaustion. For the first time, the shop felt less like a burden and more like an ally.

13 Weather with Edges

Morning arrived with a sky the color of a sharpened blade. The fog was gone; in its place, a bright, brittle light made the cobbles look like scales. Marisol felt the weather in her teeth. She unlocked the door to Ink & Ivy and waited for the bell's small mercy.

It chimed, clear, ordinary. The shop breathed, lamps warming, paper scent rising like bread. The rosette still spread across the counter under its sheet of vellum, graphite arcs faintly luminous where sunlight touched them. Finn was already there, positioned at the circle's heart as if he had slept sitting up all night.

"Shift change," Marisol murmured, stroking his head. "I'll take first watch."

Finn blinked, then stood, stretched, and stamped one neat paw onto the line where two arcs met, like a foreman approving a beam.

Her bag thumped to the floor, heavier than paper. She could feel the letter inside without touching it—*A circle closes what a hand can't.* She set the kettle going. The sound was small, domestic, and brave.

Addison arrived in a gust of hair and warmth. She held up a cloth-wrapped bundle triumphantly. "Scones! Blueberry! Don't tell the baker I cheated on him!"

Mr. Chartrand followed with his satchel and a careful gait. He looked rested; the rosette had loaned his memory back pieces of story that made his eyes bright again.

"Morning, Your Majesty," he said to Finn.

Finn bestowed a solemn blink.

They ate scones standing at the counter, crumbs dotting the vellum's edge like a constellation gone slightly off-duty. Customers drifted in: a nurse with a night-shift face, a tourist who wanted "something local but not too local," two teenagers chasing the ghost-story shelf. The kettle hummed, the register sighed, the rugs softened every step. The kingdom lived its ordinary miracle.

And still, a pressure gathered—like air right before thunder.

The bell did not chime when he came.

The front door eased open without announcing him, and the pale man stepped inside as if he owned every hinge. His coat today was a shade darker, his smile thinner, his eyes so light they seemed to have been erased and redrawn too faintly. The temperature in the shop slipped a degree; the hair on Marisol's arms lifted.

Addison went very still. Mr. Chartrand lowered his book slowly, marking his place with a business card that read *Chartrand — retired, still reading.*

"Good day," the man said, stripping the phrase of all weather. His gaze moved once across the shelves, snagged on mythology, and returned—unfailingly—to the counter.

To the rosette.

He approached without hurry. Customers, sensing something they could not name, peeled off and pretended to browse with the intensity of people hiding behind leaves.

Marisol stepped between him and the counter. "May I help you?" Her voice was the shop's voice—warm, shaped by tea, steady even when her hands weren't.

"I believe you can." His smile did not reach his eyes. "You have interfered. An untidy choice."

Finn dropped from the rosette to the counter's edge, making himself taller by intent alone. The sound he made was not a hiss; it was a resonance, a long note drawn from some instrument with strings made of nerve.

The man's gaze skated over Finn like a stone over water. "Charming."

"I'm looking," he said conversationally, "for *The Almanac of Autumn Winds* as I mentioned. Or for what remains of it." His eyes flicked toward the rosette again. "And for whatever mechanism you are using to impede natural reduction."

"We don't carry it," Marisol said, and felt the letter ghost a reply along the inside of her ribs: *He is tidy, and tidiness is not the same as care.*

"Tidy," the man repeated softly, as if tasting the word. "Yes. You see? We might understand one another. Too many redundancies on your shelves. Stories that duplicate effort. Inefficiency." He tapped his temple gently. "The mind is a finite space. Best to streamline."

Mr. Chartrand coughed, startled into boldness. "Streamline is not the same as steal."

The pale man's smile changed shape— still a smile, and yet not. "The shop has...inherited a frame." His eyes settled on the rosette. "A circle that pretends to hold time and memory. It will fail. But we needn't make an enemy of mathematics. Surrender the almanac. The rest can expire peaceably."

Addison burst out, "Books aren't milk!"

Finn's tail-stub thumped the vellum twice in the universal feline sign for *seconded.*

The man's gaze moved at last to the boy and the cat and then returned to Marisol as if he had merely glanced at punctuation. "You cannot notice what you no longer remember. What is taken becomes relief."

His hand extended—palm up, absurdly polite. "The almanac."

The seam hummed, low and furious.

Marisol put both palms flat on the counter. "No."

He did not sigh or scowl; he merely *adjusted,* as if moving a decimal. He turned and walked—soundless—into the myth aisle. As he passed, spines dulled, color leached a shade toward ash. His fingers did not touch the shelves; they seemed to erase by proximity.

"Sir." Mr. Chartrand's voice shook. "You can't—"

The man lifted one hand and made a small, economical motion, like striking a match without flame. A book slid from its place—clean, quiet—and winked out. No thud. No dust. Simply absence, tidy as a taken breath.

Addison cried, "Hey!" She ran toward the gap and grabbed at nothing. Her fingers met oak. She looked up, furious and frightened at once.

Marisol's blood ran cold. The rosette thrummed under her hands, sensing movement like a web feels a fly.

Without looking at her, the pale man said, "See? The shelf breathes easier." He made the motion again. Another book dissolved from inside the row, leaving its neighbors to lean infinitesimally closer, as if grateful.

Finn launched. He didn't leap at the man—that was not the point. He sprang to the ladder rail, ran it like a tightrope, and slammed his small body against the green spine at the seam.

The shelf clicked. The seam vibrated like a plucked wire. The rosette on the counter flared, graphite brightening to starlight and back.

The man's head turned by a fraction. "Ah," he said. "There."

"Addison!" Marisol called, her voice finding a command she didn't know she owned. "Bring the notebook. Chartrand—stand on the counter."

"Pardon?" Chartrand said, but he was already obeying, climbing with care, the old grace of a young body waking briefly in his bones. Addison slid the ledger across the rosette; the arcs shivered, aligning like a compass finding north.

Marisol grabbed her compass and, with a speed that would have made Isley blink, set the hinge and drew a new circle over the vellum, one degree tighter. Finn, tail high, placed himself dead center. The circle thrummed.

The pale man lifted his hand for a third subtraction. The book he chose trembled but did not disappear. Its title smudged, then darkened again, as if refusing to be misremembered.

He frowned—not petulantly, but with professional interest. "Containment. Inelegant, but unexpected."

"Efficient," Marisol said through her teeth, and drew another arc.

The rosette brightened. The seam hummed a note that felt like a held plank under a bare foot—steady, generous, solid. Other shelves shivered in sympathy; a memory sharpened behind Marisol's eyes, then another: *the stag etched so fine you can feel the burr of the line.* Mr. Chartrand gasped softly and put a hand to his heart.

"Enough," the man said without raising his voice. He stepped toward the counter. The air between him and the rosette thinned, as if he had made a subtraction in the space itself.

Finn's pupils blew wide. He hissed, sound bristling into every corner.

The ledger flipped on its own, pages riffling until it landed on the sketched outline of the first missing book. The air smelled briefly of pine and cold water. The ivy wallpaper rustled as if wind had found a way in sideways.

Without thinking where the thought came from, Marisol spoke a word she had not known that morning, a word that tasted like cedar and ink.

"*Hold.*"

It wasn't loud. It didn't need to be. The rosette pulsed once, a heartbeat through paper and wood. The shelf at the seam gripped itself. The gaps stopped widening.

The pale man paused, expression sharpening into interest that could have been respect in a different century. He tilted his head. "Who taught you that?"

Marisol swallowed. "A librarian." It felt true, and was. (Even if the librarian had an orchard for a reading room.)

"Mm." He glanced at Finn, whose small body now shook with a purr that had gone subsonic. "You'll discover the price. Containment is never free."

Addison, voice small but unbroken, said, "We'll pay it. Not you."

He watched her for one long, subtractive second, and then looked back at Marisol. "I'll return," he said, as if announcing the weather. "You cannot circle the horizon. And winter is efficient."

He turned and left.

This time, the bell did chime. It sounded tired.

The shop breathed out all at once. A customer exhaled audibly from behind New Releases, startled to find he had been holding his breath through a conversation he hadn't understood. The teenagers giggled nervously and fled. The nurse bought a paperback as if purchasing a charm.

Mr. Chartrand climbed carefully down. His hands shook. "That man," he said softly, "has never learned the difference between pruning and erasing."

Addison put both palms on the rosette. "Did we really—did you—?"

Marisol could feel the circle still humming, quieter now, a warm ring pressed into the grain of the counter. She could feel the seam, too, subdued but awake. She nodded. "For now."

Finn stepped out of the circle, walked to the end of the counter, and threw himself dramatically into Marisol's arms. He hooked one paw over her shoulder and pressed his face under her chin with the authority of a hero accepting medals.

She laughed, breathless and wobbly. "Co-architect," she whispered into his fur.

He purred so hard her teeth buzzed.

When the last customer left and the lamps lowered, they took stock. The ledger showed two new outlines—and two that had darkened where the circle had pulled memory back into them. Net loss: unclear. Net defiance: measurable.

Chartrand poured the dregs of the coffee into three cups. They drank it like a spell needs salt.

"Price," he said after a time, tasting the word with care. "The man wasn't wrong about that."

Addison set her jaw. "We choose it, though. That's the rule."

Marisol thought of the letter's line: *Pay it with a memory you can spare but will miss.* She thought of the way her mother's laugh sounded over the phone when a recipe went sideways. Of summers by the lake pocketing stones. Of a childhood birthday when a neighbor's dog had decided she was his person for one whole afternoon.

She put her palm on the vellum. "Not tonight," she told the circle. "But soon."

Finn, as if understanding that she had just put her hand on a scale—even a little— re-centered himself at the rosette's heart and closed his eyes. His purr rumbled like a cornerstone settling.

They locked the door together. Mr. Chartrand touched the seam with two fingers, a benediction. Addison taped a handwritten sign near the register that said, in blocky, earnest letters: *WE ARE HERE.* She drew a tiny cat face beside it.

Upstairs, Marisol rolled fresh vellum. This time, the circles came first, then the walls. She drew a lobby that wanted to be a story and a shop that wanted to be a building, and somewhere between them, she recognized herself.

Finn stood on the sill, watching the street's thin line of silver until it went dark. When he finally returned to the drafting table, he placed one paw gently on her wrist, guiding—not pushing.

"Okay," she said, to the cat, to the circle, to whatever listened behind the wood. "Tomorrow we make the circle bigger."

Finn purred once, an approving thrum.

Below them, in the quiet kingdom, the shelves settled. Somewhere in Mythology, a spine brightened a shade back toward its true color. The rosette on the counter kept its watch like a lantern that had learned the trick of burning without smoke.

Outside, the weather sharpened again. Winter thought about its efficiencies. The pale man considered his next subtraction.

But inside, for now, the circle held.

And the cat did not sleep.

Ink & Ivy breathed in sleep. The lamps were dark, the rugs settled, the ivy wallpaper lay still. Upstairs, Marisol dozed fitfully, dreaming of circles and missing books.

But at midnight, the bell gave a soundless swing. The door did not open, yet cold air slid across the threshold. A shadow lengthened along the mythology aisle, clean-edged and pale.

The man did not enter fully—his shape was the idea of him, the subtraction he carried. He reached not with hands but with intent. Three books quivered on their spines. Their titles blurred like chalk in rain.

The rosette on the counter flared faintly, arcs pulsing, graphite glowing like moonlit steel. The circle held the shelves in place, a barrier drawn in stubborn pencil. The man's shadow paused, as if testing glass.

Finn, who had been curled on the counter, lifted his head. His eyes caught the shimmer and burned green as sea glass. He stood, tail high, and let out a sound so low it was more vibration than voice. The rosette answered with a hum that resonated in the wood.

The shadow thinned, retreated, slid back under the door. The bell gave a half-jingle, then stilled.

Finn sat watching the rest of the night, unblinking.

When the hour turned toward dawn, Finn left the counter. He padded into the aisles on silent paws, his round body weaving gracefully among the stacks.

In Gardening, he rubbed his cheek against a book on roses. In Poetry, he batted gently at the dangling ribbon of an anthology. In History, he sat neatly before a row of atlases as if commanding them to hold their shape.

He stopped longest in Mythology. The seam quivered faintly, like a door dreaming of being opened. Finn pressed both paws against it and pushed—not enough to move wood, but enough to remind it that he was watching.

A page slipped free from the shelf above, fluttering down. Finn pinned it with one paw, studied it solemnly, then dragged it to the counter. When Marisol found it hours later, she would see faint words describing a winter wind that moved sideways.

For now, Finn settled at the rosette's edge, curling his body into a crescent that completed the geometry. His purr spread like mortar through the shelves.

Marisol woke before dawn, the kind of waking that feels summoned. She found Finn on the counter, the stray page beneath his paw, the rosette faintly glowing.

Her chest tightened. She remembered the letter: *Pay it with a memory you can spare but will miss.*

She sat at the counter and laid both palms flat on the vellum. "If we don't give, it takes. Better I choose."

She closed her eyes. A thousand small memories pressed forward: summers by the lake, Addison's laughter, Mr. Chartrand's voice reading aloud, her grandmother's kitchen, the smell of ink on her first drafting set.

Her throat ached. She searched for something she could spare but would miss.

Finally, she found it: the memory of her first bike ride without training wheels. She remembered the wobble, the scrape on her knee, her father's cheer behind her. She had carried it like a badge. But perhaps she could let it go.

She whispered it into the circle: "Take this one. But let the others stay."

The vellum warmed under her hands. The arcs pulsed once. The memory slid from her like water slipping from skin—no pain, just absence. She knew the ride had happened. She remembered the story of it. But the feeling of wind in her hair was gone, replaced with a hollow she could not fill.

Her eyes burned. She laughed once, softly, at the strangeness. "A memory tithe," she said. "So be it."

Finn leaned into her arm, purr steady, as though assuring her she had chosen well.

By the time Addison and Chartrand arrived, the shop glowed as though nothing had happened. Customers trickled in, bringing chatter and damp umbrellas.

Marisol smiled, poured tea, and passed scones.

But her eyes lingered on the rosette. She could feel it: a little stronger, a little sharper, fed by what she had given.

She whispered her benediction with new weight that evening: "Goodnight, little kingdom. Hold together."

The seam hummed back, not warning, not sigh, but gratitude.

And Finn, who had patrolled the shelves, driven off the shadow, and witnessed her tithe, curled in the circle once more, a guardian shaped like a cat, carrying secrets in his fur.

14 The Floor Drawn True

They met before opening, the shop still wearing its morning hush like a shawl. Marisol laid her tools on the counter with the tenderness of setting out teacups: chalk, twine, a carpenter's compass borrowed from the firm, her three lake stones, a soft cloth, a carpenter's pencil worn to a friendly nub. Finn hopped up, nosed each item, then sat with the proprietary air of a site supervisor.

Mr. Chartrand arrived with a folding ruler and a roll of butcher paper. "In case the wood objects," he said, patting the counter as if soothing an old horse.

Addison burst in with a tote clinking faintly. "Painter's tape and knee pads," she announced. "And snacks." She produced a pack of shortbread like a magician revealing doves. "I Googled chalk circle tips, but I think the internet has never met Finn."

Finn pretended not to hear and stamped one paw on the vellum rosette, as if to say: promote me to floor plan, please.

They rolled back the rugs in the central aisles, revealing floorboards burnished by years of steps. The wood exhaled a faint sweetness—old pine and dust warmed by stories.

"Center?" Marisol said softly. She set the lake stones in her palm, feeling their cool weight. The letter's rules thrummed under her skin: *Hexagon at the heart. A circle closes what a hand can't.*

Finn leapt from the counter and padded to the spot where mythology met classics. He turned three tight circles, then sat, tail-stub tapping once. Foreman's choice.

"Center," Marisol agreed.

They worked in comfortable silence, moving like people who had shared a kitchen for years. Addison snapped blue painter's tape into a soft hexagon that hugged Finn's chosen center. Mr. Chartrand measured the aisles, calling out numbers with the pleased certainty of a man reuniting with arithmetic. Marisol knelt, chalk in hand, and anchored the twine to a nail she'd gently introduced to the floor years ago for holiday garlands, now pressed into grander service.

"Radius?" Chartrand asked.

Marisol took a breath. "From seam to counter's edge. One degree smaller than last night." She looked up and found Finn already planted on the twine's free end, pinning it like a necessary punctuation mark.

"Thank you," she murmured. He blinked at her, saintly.

She drew. Chalk lifted and whispered; circle bloomed out from center, smooth and steady, wrapping the counter, brushing the foot of Biography, passing through Local

History like an embrace. The line met itself clean as a kiss.

Addison clapped once, then caught herself and mouthed *sorry!* to the floor.

They added arcs at one-degree turns, rosette unfolding across the boards: petals of chalk overlapping in soft geometry, each curve passing through the taped hexagon's corners, each intersection aligning with an absence in Marisol's ledger. The pattern rose not above the floor but *within* it, as if coaxing something the wood had been saving.

"Beautiful," Chartrand whispered.

The ivy wallpaper rustled, approving.

The bell chimed: early birds braving the bright cold. A pair of teachers in the mood for poetry; a contractor in mud-caked boots who wanted a thriller; the baker with a paper bag and a grin. They stopped on the threshold, staring at the chalk rosette sprawled like lace.

"Renovating?" the contractor asked, bemused.

"Story maintenance," Addison said gravely, offering him a strip of painter's tape to step over the line.

The teachers watched Finn march the circumference and, without a word, lifted their skirts and tiptoed along the chalk's outside edge as though entering a chapel.

The baker passed the bag to Mr. Chartrand. "For rites," he said, eyes gone soft.

Marisol kept moving, adjusting arcs, cleaning smudges with the soft cloth, chalk dust ghosting her palms. When a customer needed a recommendation, she rose to press a book into their hands and then dropped back into the circle the way a pianist returns to the keys between conversations.

Finn managed the traffic, stationing himself where the chalk was most vulnerable, redirecting ankles with dignified shoulder bumps. He let a toddler pat his head exactly three times before gliding out of reach as if he'd been poured.

"Good boy," Marisol said to him under her breath. "Best boy."

He pretended not to hear and sat on the exact point where the seam's hum was strongest.

Near noon, a college student—apologetic, flustered, backpack bristling with dangling cords—stepped backward from Graphic Novels and scuffed a shoe across the rosette. The chalk line smeared, breaking the circle into a hesitant curve.

The seam thrummed, off-key.

"It's okay," the student blurted, mortified. "I can—do you have—?"

"Don't move," Marisol said, gentle but urgent. She knelt, cloth in one hand, chalk in the other, and breathed herself quiet. Finn pressed to her side, warm against her calf. Addison crouched opposite, holding the painter's tape square, steady as a surgeon's assistant. Mr. Chartrand's palm rested lightly on the floorboard as if lending pulse.

Marisol redrew the arc, feathering from the unbroken segment to the smudge until the line remembered itself. The chalk whispered its way back into place. The seam eased. The rosette exhaled.

The student's shoulders dropped. "Magic circle?" they asked, half-joking, half-afraid.

"Structure," Chartrand said. "And kindness."

The student nodded like someone filing away an important definition. "I'll walk around," they said, and did.

With the outer circle secured, they moved to the hinge: the slender chalk bridge that would link counter to seam. Marisol chalked it last, hand steady, mouth dry. Finn set one paw at the bridge's midpoint and closed his eyes, purring deep.

The floor warmed beneath her knees. The ivy wallpaper rustled as though midnight wind had found a noon path. Somewhere in Folklore, a book slid forward an inch and then settled, as if correcting its posture.

"Do you feel—" Addison began.

"Yes," Marisol said, breath catching. The hum threaded through her bones, not fierce, not loud—present. The kind of sound you trust because you've known it your whole life without knowing its name.

A woman near Local History wiped her eyes and couldn't explain why.

Mr. Chartrand whispered a poem to himself, something about circles not beginning or ending, about returning to the place and knowing it for the first time. The words fell into the rosette and stayed, quiet ballast.

When the lunch wave ebbed, they tested. Addison slid her ledger into the circle; the squares of absence darkened at the edges, as if ink had come home. Mr. Chartrand placed his twine-bound notebook on the bridge; a paragraph returned to him, the scent of lake water rising like steam. He smiled without showing his teeth, a smile that started in the eyes and warmed outward.

Marisol did not look at the ledger. Instead, she set her palm on the seam's edge.

"Hold," she said—Keeper's word, learned in a dream and a letter and a life she hadn't known she was living.

The chalk brightened, incredibly, impossibly, not with light but with *attention*. The shop listened back. The circle didn't cage the aisles; it *joined* them. The hum went from "beneath" to "among."

Finn opened his eyes and yawned, then—shameless—rolled onto his back right across the bridge, paws in the air, throat bared, purr roaring like a small engine. Laughter loosened every shoulder in the room.

"Chief inspector approves," Addison declared.

"Then I'll file the paperwork," Chartrand said, and solemnly ate a shortbread.

As shadows lengthened, Marisol felt the circle asking—not a demand, not a hunger; an honest cost. The letter's line arose again: *The shop will take a tithe, but you may choose the currency.*

She looked at Addison, at Chartrand, at Finn sprawled like a saint. "Small," she said softly. "Shared." She took a breath. "I'll give a memory of a taste. Lemon bars, the recipe from sophomore year. I'll remember that they were good, but not exactly why."

Addison swallowed, then squared her shoulders. "I'll give...the color of the sweater I wore the first day I came here. Only that. Not the feeling."

Chartrand placed a hand over his heart. "I will give a single line from a mediocre poem I used to like too much." His eyes crinkled. "The shop deserves better lines."

They stood within the rosette, each with one palm to the chalk. Not a ceremony, a simple act. The floor warmed; the air shifted; the given things slid away cleanly, clean as tidying a desk.

None of them swayed. All of them breathed easier.

Finn hopped to the seam, touched it with his forehead, then returned to the center, proud as a mason tasting mortar he has mixed himself.

At closing, the rosette lay soft and steadfast across the boards. Marisol swept gently around it, chalk dust rising like pale incense. The day's last customers left with books hugged to chests and bewildered smiles they didn't try to understand.

They lowered the lamps. The ivy wallpaper stilled. The seam hummed a note that sounded, to Marisol's ear, like relief.

She whispered her benediction, the words older now that she knew their weight. "Goodnight, little kingdom. Hold together."

Finn leapt to her shoulder, pressing his face to her jaw, purr so deep it stitched throat to heart. Addison locked the till; Chartrand flipped the sign. They lingered a moment longer, three people and a cat and a chalk-drawn geometry that had become a promise.

Outside, winter tested the glass with a cool breath. Inside, the circle held.

And somewhere in the orchard that lives sideways from weather, a Keeper lifted her head and smiled, as if she'd felt a small circle traced true a long way off.

15 Winter's First Knock

By day, Marisol's pencil should have been steady. She sat at her drafting table in the firm's office, tracing lobby revisions, annotating stair angles, and noting fire code clearances. Isley hovered nearby, tapping his pen against her vellum with a rhythm that grated.

"These curves again," he said, squinting at her plans. "You've got to think linear. Circulation works best with straight spines."

Spines. The word made her stomach tighten.

She tried to erase a circle she'd drawn into the atrium's ceiling, but the graphite blurred rather than vanished, reasserting itself no matter how hard she rubbed. When she shifted her angle, she saw faint rosette lines hovering like watermarks.

The office printer jammed with a sound eerily like the seam's hum. The fluorescent lights flickered as though the shop's pulse had threaded into this too-ordinary place.

"Take a break, Callan," Isley said, exasperated. "You look like you've been up all night."

She had. But not here.

Her gaze drifted to her notebook on the corner of the desk. She'd tucked it under client folders, but even hidden, she could feel its weight tugging her like gravity.

At lunch, instead of eating, she traced one small circle on her blotter with the side of her pencil. It glowed faintly before fading. Isley didn't notice, but Finn would have.

After work, she hurried back to Ink & Ivy. The chalk circle sprawled across the floor as they had left it, faint smudges betraying where customers had stepped but still coherent, still humming. Addison had taped up a sign: *WALK WITH CARE— MAGIC UNDERFOOT* in block letters decorated with stars.

Finn sat at the seam, tail flicking, as if he'd been appointed watchman by a council of shelves.

"Did he come back?" Marisol asked softly.

Finn chirruped, hopped down, and trotted toward Folklore. A book lay skewed forward, as though nudged halfway from its row but then shoved back. A warning or a failed theft.

Addison emerged from the stacks, a smear of chalk on her cheek. "I think he tried. But the circle held. Finn was doing laps all night, like a cat security guard."

Mr. Chartrand joined them, carrying a tray of mugs. "Not laps," he corrected gently. "A perimeter." He handed Marisol tea that smelled faintly of sage. "Even guardians have a strategy."

Finn leapt to the counter, landed with a solid thump, and tipped his head back as if to say, *They understand nothing.*

That evening, frost feathered the inside of the shop windows, though the heat was running. The air was a bit colder between the aisles, especially near Mythology. When Addison reached for a Norse saga, her breath puffed white.

"He's close," she whispered.

The seam hummed nervously. The chalk lines dimmed at one corner where a heel had smudged them earlier. Marisol knelt, cloth in hand, to repair it, but her chalk crumbled into powder.

"Try this." Chartrand passed her his fountain pen, the ink black-blue and shining.

She hesitated, then bent and drew a fresh arc with ink. It sank into the grain of the floorboards and held, darker than chalk, as if permanent.

The hum steadied. The frost melted back into droplets.

Finn pounced on the droplets, batting them into nonexistence, then strutted as if he'd solved the climate crisis personally.

A steady trickle of patrons entered that night, each unconsciously drawn to the circle's glow. An elderly woman paused on its edge and whispered, "It feels like church." A boy no older than nine sat cross-legged in the middle, nose buried in a dragon compendium, refusing to leave until his mother bribed him with cocoa.

Addison whispered to Marisol, "They can *feel* it, even if they don't know."

Marisol nodded. "Which means he can too."

As if on cue, the bell jangled without a hand on it. The door remained shut. A hush rolled through the shop, settling like dust.

Finn arched, tail bristling. The seam shuddered.

The pale man did not enter. Instead, words on the spines nearest the seam began to dim. Letters thinned, fading into indecipherable scratches.

Addison gasped. "He's erasing from the outside."

Marisol grabbed the ledger. She sketched the fading titles, each rectangle vibrating in her pencil lines. "Circle's not wide enough," she whispered.

Chartrand pressed both palms to the floor. "Then we must widen it. Not later. Now."

They scrambled: Addison fetching chalk, Chartrand unrolling butcher paper to test extensions, Marisol calculating radii with her compass. Finn darted between them, stamping paws at weak points like an engineer pointing out stress fractures.

The spines flickered—dim, brighten, dim again—as though the circle fought against subtraction.

Marisol whispered the Keeper's word— "*Hold*"—and traced a larger arc. The chalk flared, connected, steadied.

The words on the spines snapped back into clarity.

But the pale man's laughter, thin and dry as paper rubbed between fingers, echoed faintly through the aisles.

When the hum settled, Marisol knew the shop was asking again. Not gently this time. Payment for what they had just won.

"I'll do it," she said quickly. "I already gave one memory. I can give more."

"No," Chartrand said sharply. "Not only you." He placed a trembling hand on the ledger. "I will give the name of my first classroom. I will still remember teaching. But the walls, the number above the door— I'll let those go."

Addison bit her lip. "I'll give...my favorite video game level. Just one. I'll still have the rest."

Marisol swallowed, then added, "I'll give the taste of my grandmother's stew. I'll remember the warmth, the way she ladled it. But not the taste."

Together, they laid hands on the chalk. The hum deepened, the lines pulsed. Each memory slid gently out, leaving a clean hollow where it had been.

Finn pressed his forehead to Marisol's hand. His purr filled the absence, softened it.

The circle brightened, sharper than before. The spines stayed whole.

By closing, they were exhausted. Addison slumped on the counter, Chartrand's pen smudged ink across his cuff, and Marisol's fingers trembled around her compass.

But the circle held.

Customers left humming tunes they couldn't explain, eyes brighter than when they entered. The ivy wallpaper stilled, satisfied. The seam's hum became a soft lullaby.

Marisol whispered the benediction, voice cracked but steady. "Goodnight, little kingdom. Hold together."

The shop sighed in return.

And Finn, exhausted but smug, sprawled in the exact center of the enlarged rosette, paws splayed, whiskers twitching, his purr like a metronome marking the rhythm of a kingdom not yet lost.

16 Signs Within

Morning came soft and misty. The circle sprawled across Ink & Ivy's floor, chalk lines dulled by last night's battle but still intact. Customers stepped gingerly around it, guided by Addison's signs and Finn's strategic bumps to shins.

Marisol knelt at the center once the shop quieted. "It's holding," she murmured. "But not enough. He laughed at us."

Mr. Chartrand perched on a stool, sipping tea. "Circles are frames. Strong frames, yes, but frames only. Without what's inside, they're empty rooms."

Addison tilted her head, notebook in her lap. "Then we decorate the room."

Marisol looked up sharply. "Symbols."

Chartrand nodded slowly. "Meaning is mortar."

Finn padded into the center of the rosette and flopped dramatically onto his side. He stretched until his stub-tail thumped the floor inside the chalk petals. When he rolled onto his back, paws in the air, he looked exactly like punctuation waiting for a sentence.

"Yes," Marisol said softly. "Symbols. Stories. We need the sentences."

They spent the morning pulling books that might serve as lexicons: runes from *The*

Elder Futhark, glyphs from *Egyptian Myths*, sigils from a half-forgotten occult primer in Folklore. Addison stacked them like an altar on the counter.

"We'll test them," she said, eyes shining. "See which the shop accepts."

Mr. Chartrand raised a hand. "Careful. A library has memory of its own. Not every sign will harmonize."

They spread vellum across a small side table. Marisol traced simple forms, spirals, stars, and interlocking triangles, while Addison sketched jagged glyphs in pencil, her handwriting surprisingly elegant. Chartrand copied a single rune with painstaking care, ink blotted like a heartbeat.

Finn watched from the chair back, tail flicking, ready to veto.

Marisol chose a spiral, chalking it inside the circle near the seam. The line glowed faintly, humming in harmony with the rosette. A book two shelves down sighed and slid half an inch straighter.

"Accepted," Chartrand murmured.

Encouraged, Addison added a jagged glyph at the circle's edge. The chalk darkened, edges fraying, and the seam trembled uneasily. A book vanished in a snap of displaced air.

"Rejected," Finn growled, darting forward to swipe the glyph with his paw until it blurred into harmless dust.

Addison flushed. "Sorry. Wrong language."

"Not wrong," Chartrand corrected gently. "Just not ours."

It was Finn who made the next move. He padded into the center, crouched low, and with his paw traced a crude shape in chalk dust: a small circle, bisected once, with three dots arranged like whiskers.

Marisol laughed softly. "That's...a cat's face."

But the chalk shimmered, glowing brighter than her careful spiral. The seam's hum steadied, deepened. Several faint gaps in the ledger darkened, their outlines sharper.

Addie whooped. "Of course, the cat knows the right sigil!"

Chartrand smiled, eyes misty. "Every temple has its familiar. Some temples are wise enough to let the familiar lead."

Marisol bent to copy Finn's paw-mark neatly, making it permanent in chalk. "Your symbol, then," she whispered to him. "Our keeper's mark."

Finn purred like an organ chord, rolling once across the sigil to seal it.

Late afternoon, Mr. Chartrand suggested trying ink instead of chalk. "Chalk fades. Ink endures."

Marisol hesitated, fountain pen poised over the floorboards. "Endures...and costs."

She chose a simple rune for memory—drawn in careful black lines at the circle's heart beside Finn's sigil. The air thickened, heavy as humid summer. Her notebook rattled open on its own.

One outline inside—the first book that had vanished—darkened fully, details filling in. She saw its title: *The Almanac of Autumn Winds*. She gasped, running her fingers over the name.

But something slipped in return. She couldn't recall her old drafting professor's face anymore—only the rasp of his voice. The memory had gone, tidy as subtraction.

Addison's eyes widened. "It worked." Then she softened. "But it hurt, didn't it?"

Marisol nodded. "The shop demands ink. Chalk isn't enough."

Finn pressed close, his purr wrapping around the hollow she'd given up, cushioning it.

By nightfall, the circle bloomed with symbols: Marisol's spirals, Chartrand's rune for story, Finn's paw-mark. Each glowed faintly, pulsing in rhythm with the seam. The air of the shop had changed—still cozy, still book-scented, but layered with something reverent, as though they were inside a cathedral whose hymn was paper.

Customers wandered in, unaware yet visibly softened. A man with a weary face walked out humming. A mother bought three picture books, though she'd only come for one. A girl hugged her poetry volume as though it might shield her heart.

After closing, the three of them sat cross-legged inside the rosette, mugs of tea steaming between their knees. Addison lit a candle stub and placed it at Finn's sigil.

"To the circle," she said.

"To the kingdom," Chartrand added.

"To holding," Marisol whispered.

Finn yawned, lay himself across all three of their ankles, and purred until the chalk itself seemed to vibrate with his approval.

17 Counter-Signs

The morning was ordinary until it wasn't. Customers came for thrillers, for local cookbooks, for children's picture books. Addison manned the till, Chartrand traced call numbers in his notebook, and Marisol guided a young man to Architecture. Finn sprawled, languid, across the counter, tail-stub twitching in rhythm with the hum of the rosette.

Then the chalk spirals shifted. Not broke—not smudged—but bent. Their lines twisted into sharper angles, as if a hand had tugged them into shapes more efficient, less kind.

The seam groaned. A book popped forward and fell, landing on its spine with a startled crack. Customers looked up, uneasy.

Marisol ran to the rosette, kneeling hard enough to bruise. "He's rewriting them."

Mr. Chartrand squinted. "See—the curves shaved flat, the spirals squared. His marks are subtraction in disguise."

Finn leapt down, planting himself on the warped spiral, pawing at it furiously until chalk dust flew. His hiss filled the shop. The line recoiled faintly but held its new, sterile form.

Marisol whispered the Keeper's word: *"Hold."*

The spiral flickered, oscillating between her curve and his angle, like a coin spinning on its edge.

It escalated quickly. Her spiral fractured into a triangle, his rune bent into a subtraction sign, Addison's attempted star warped into a tidy grid. The shop shuddered; the ivy wallpaper crisped at the edges, as though drying in heat.

"He's inside the language," Chartrand said grimly. "Turning sign to symbol, symbol to subtraction."

Addison snatched a stick of chalk and drew a quick heart beside the rosette. The chalk flared, faltered, nearly folded into a zero.

"No!" Marisol grabbed her wrist. "Not raw shapes—story."

She seized her compass, set it trembling on the wood, and sketched a circle around Finn's sigil, the whiskered face he'd drawn in dust. The chalk held. The circle wrapped his mark in protection, amplifying its hum.

Finn purred so loudly it sounded like defiance.

The warped symbols buckled, snapping back toward curves, though faint cracks remained where his subtraction had bitten.

The duel rippled outward. A teenager browsing Fantasy blinked in confusion, unable to recall which book she'd just pulled.

A man in Biography frowned, saying he'd been reading the same page for five minutes without comprehension.

Marisol's stomach knotted. The fight wasn't abstract—it was leaking into memory.

"Anchor them," Chartrand said, voice trembling but sure. "Give them a story to stand on."

Addison darted to the counter, grabbed a poetry anthology, and began reading aloud. Her voice quavered but steadied as the words filled the shop. "...*the circle is not the end but the beginning again...*"

The rosette pulsed in time with her voice. Customers blinked, shoulders relaxing, as if tugged back to themselves.

The pale man's symbols twitched, buckled, then pressed harder, turning Addison's spoken words into faint scratch marks at the edge of the circle, trying to erase them before they reached the air.

Finn sprang into her lap, head butting the book, claws snagging pages until Addison's laughter broke free. The sound cracked the erasure. The marks dissolved.

Mr. Chartrand stepped forward, surprising them all. He drew a rune of his own across the floor: not borrowed from a lexicon this time, but one he made from memory—a shape of a teacher's desk, a chalkboard, rows of eager faces.

He pressed his hand to it. "This is mine," he whispered. "You can't subtract what has already been shared."

The rune flared bright gold. The pale man's counter-symbol tried to flatten it into a rectangle, tidy and bare. Chartrand's line refused. It thickened, branching outward like veins, binding itself to shelves where his students' names still lived in marginalia of donated books.

The shop hummed louder.

Marisol felt tears in her throat. Chartrand's rune wasn't efficient, but it was alive. That was its strength.

The duel reached its peak. Spirals flickered, runes twisted, glyphs warred. Marisol pressed both palms to the floor, whispering the Keeper's word again and again—*Hold. Hold. Hold.*

At last, the ivy wallpaper stirred, leaves trembling as though in the wind. A faint voice, not audible, but known, threaded through Marisol's bones: *You are not alone.*

The shop itself added its mark. A crack in the floorboard sealed, its grain curling into a spiral that mirrored hers. The ivy leaves etched a faint sigil across the wall, shaped like an open book.

The pale man's angles recoiled, faltered, and faded, retreating like smoke drawn back through a chimney.

The seam settled with a soft hum. The shelves leaned back into place. Customers blinked, looked around, and resumed browsing as if nothing had happened.

Addison dropped her chalk and sagged into a chair, cheeks flushed. Chartrand sat heavily beside her, notebook clutched in his hand.

Marisol slumped to the counter, head in her arms, heart pounding.

Finn strutted to the center of the rosette, sat tall, and licked one paw delicately as if nothing unusual had occurred—heroism, after all, should not be made into a fuss.

Addison groaned. "I hate him. The pale man. He doesn't just take books. He takes *meaning*."

Chartrand nodded. "Subtraction masquerading as order. It looks clean until you notice the gaps."

Marisol whispered, still trembling: "And he'll come again."

Finn hopped onto her shoulder, rubbing his face against her jawline. His purr vibrated steady reassurance: *Yes. But so will we.*

They locked up late, leaving the chalk and ink to cool on the floor. Marisol pressed her palm to the rosette, whispered the benediction: "Goodnight, little kingdom. Hold together."

Addie added, "Don't let him in."

Chartrand placed his hand over both of theirs. "Remember: we answer subtraction with a story."

Finn curled at the center of the circle once more, eyes slitting shut, his body the punctuation that ended the sentence and began it again.

Outside, the frost thickened. Inside, the symbols glowed faintly, alive and stubborn.

The duel was only the beginning.

18 Subtracted Weather

It began with silence. No birdsong at dawn, no tires hissing on wet streets, no kettle whistle in neighboring apartments. Marisol woke to a white-gray windowpane, frost feathering the edges from *inside*.

By the time she reached Ink & Ivy, the storm had begun in earnest. Not a blizzard, not rain, something between. Flakes fell but made no sound when they hit the cobblestones. The air smelled not of snow but absence, like paper left too long in the sun.

Addison huddled by the counter with her coat still on, cheeks red. "It's weird," she whispered. "The snow doesn't melt on you. It just...vanishes." She held up her mitten. Perfectly dry.

Mr. Chartrand arrived moments later, breath fogging in bursts. He carried a stack of children's books like a shield. "He's reached for the weather now. Subtraction doesn't stop at shelves."

The seam hummed low, nervous. Finn leapt onto the counter and stamped twice, as if declaring roll call. His green eyes were wide, unblinking.

The shop's wide windows frosted over, not with filigree but with blank whiteness, as though painted shut. Streetlamps outside blurred into pale smudges. Footsteps of passersby left no sound.

Inside, customers moved quietly, voices dim. A boy clutching a dinosaur encyclopedia frowned. "Why can't I hear myself talk?"

His mother shushed him automatically, but her own words came out muted, almost erased.

Marisol's heart hammered. She ran to the rosette and dropped to her knees. The chalk spirals were faint, edges dulling as if frost were leaching their warmth.

"He's trying to mute us," she said. "To erase the shop's sound."

Addison clutched her ledger. "If he erases sound, he erases story."

Chartrand pressed his palms to the floorboards. "We must answer with noise. With voice."

Finn meowed, a sharp, defiant yowl that cut the air like chalk squeaking on a board. For a moment, the rosette brightened.

They scrambled. Addison began reading aloud from her favorite fantasy trilogy, words tumbling fast. Mr. Chartrand recited a poem by heart, voice trembling but sure. Marisol added her own, pulling a book of architectural essays, speaking passages about arches, columns, vaults, structures that endured storms.

Customers joined, confused but willing. One woman read a recipe aloud, voice wobbling over tablespoons and teaspoons. A man whispered the lyrics of a song he half-remembered. A child sang the alphabet in a proud shout.

The shop filled with layered voices, messy and imperfect. The chalk symbols glowed, spirals curling brighter, Finn's whisker-mark shimmering steady as a heartbeat.

The frost on the windows cracked slightly, letting in the faintest color of lamplight. Outside, the snow hissed angrily against the glass, not silent anymore but sharp.

Marisol whispered, almost to herself: "We're louder than subtraction."

Finn leapt down and began his patrol, weaving the aisles. At each section, he stopped, planted his paw on a book, and meowed once. Gardening. Romance. Mystery. His voice carried, thin but piercing, stitching sound into silence.

In Mythology, he did not meow but growled a long, low vibration that rattled the shelves. The seam steadied. Books that had been trembling settled back into place.

Customers smiled nervously, some clapping as though Finn were performing.

The sound of palms meeting palms echoed, multiplied, and filled the room with warmth.

Marisol wiped her eyes. "Good boy. Best boy."

Finn strutted back to the rosette, tail high, and flopped into the center with a satisfied thud. His purr reverberated, a low drum against the storm.

The windows thinned for a heartbeat. Through the frost, Marisol saw him. The pale man stood in the whiteness, untouched by snow, coat immaculate. His eyes were pale blanks, fixed on the shop.

He raised one hand. A gust of subtraction struck the glass. Letters on the spines nearest the window blurred.

Marisol shouted, "*Hold!*"

The circle answered, symbols glowing, Finn yowling. The blurred letters sharpened again, though faint cracks ran through them like spiderwebs.

The man's lips moved, though no sound carried: *You cannot shout forever.*

Then he turned, and the storm thickened until he was gone.

When the storm eased, the circle pulsed, asking. The air is thick with need.

Marisol looked to Chartrand and Addison. "It wants more. Payment for what we kept."

Chartrand sighed. "Then we give." He touched his chest. "I'll surrender the exact date of my retirement. I'll remember leaving, but not the day."

Addison bit her lip. "I'll give the name of the first boy I had a crush on. Just that. Nothing else."

Marisol closed her eyes. The warmth of her grandmother's stew was already gone. The bike ride too. She pressed her palm to the rosette. "I'll give the smell of my drafting pencils. I'll still draw. But the scent will be gone."

The rosette flared. The cost slid cleanly away, tidy as subtraction but chosen, and therefore gentler. The shop steadied.

Finn pressed his head against Marisol's palm, purr filling the hollow she hadn't realized would ache so much.

By closing, the storm had thinned. Snow lay on rooftops, but footsteps crunched audibly again. The frost on the windows had melted to harmless beads.

Customers left with books hugged close. A child waved solemnly to Finn. A teacher thanked Chartrand for "the strangest but most comforting story hour I've ever been in."

They tidied together. Addison taped another hand-lettered sign: *LOUD VOICES WELCOME*. Chartrand shelved returns with reverence. Marisol swept chalk dust, whispering her benediction: "Goodnight, little kingdom. Hold together."

The shop hummed back. Finn curled at the seam, tail tucked, eyes half-closed, purr deep as winter hearth fire.

Outside, the pale man's storm retreated, leaving the air brittle but alive. Inside, Ink & Ivy's circle of symbols glowed faintly, stubborn as hope.

19 Lines that Don't Belong

Marisol spread her lobby plans across the drafting table at the firm. The vellum crinkled under her palms. She'd redrawn the atrium three times, each iteration stubbornly curving into arcs that felt right even when the code demanded angles.

The new elevator shaft? Its outline bent ever so slightly toward a spiral. The mezzanine rail? It repeated in whisker-like slashes. She had not drawn them consciously, but the marks persisted, faint as ghost watermarks under the lead.

Her stomach fluttered. Symbols from the rosette had bled onto her blueprints.

"Marisol." Isley loomed over her shoulder, tie askew, mug in hand. He tapped the vellum. "What's this curve? It wastes square footage. This whole section—" he jabbed at the rosette-like atrium— "what's it even supposed to be?"

She swallowed. "Flow. Circulation. A lobby should invite movement, not box it."

Isley frowned, tilting his head. "You're starting to sound like a poet, not a drafter. Clients don't pay for metaphors."

Marisol forced a smile. "I'll redraw." But her pencil hand twitched, aching to trace a circle instead.

Two days later, the meeting came. She carried rolled vellum into the boardroom, heart pounding. Three clients sat waiting—suits, pens, polite smiles sharpened for critique. Isley introduced her briskly, gesturing to the plans unfurled across the table.

The men leaned in, murmuring. "Unusual curvature," one said. "Feels organic. Not typical for downtown."

Another frowned, tapping the mezzanine. "This motif—see these whisker-like marks? Is this intentional detailing?"

Heat rose in Marisol's cheeks. "Just...an ornamental note," she lied. "We can adjust."

They exchanged glances. "Unorthodox," one muttered, "but oddly compelling. Like it wants to pull people inward."

Isley shot her a sharp look. "We'll refine."

Her pulse raced. She knew what they were seeing: the shop's geometry bled into her professional lines. Sigils masquerading as ornaments.

At lunch, Marisol hid in the breakroom, sipping stale coffee. She pulled her notebook from her bag, flipping to the ledger. The gaps throbbed faintly, each one tethered to a symbol she'd traced at Ink & Ivy.

Her drafting life and the shop's survival were no longer separate. The pale man's subtraction gnawed at both.

She whispered to herself, almost in prayer: "I can't lose one world to save the other."

The door swung open. A junior drafter poked his head in. "Hey, Marisol? Weird question. Your plans—did you use some kind of sacred geometry trick? They feel...different. Like they hum."

She stared, throat dry. "Hum?"

"Yeah. Don't worry, it's cool." He shrugged, grabbing a soda. "Kind of makes me want to linger in the lobby. Like it's...holding me."

He left.

Marisol pressed her face to her hands, whispering: "Oh, no."

That evening, she hurried to Ink & Ivy. Addison was sprawled across the counter doing homework, Chartrand shelving biographies with methodical reverence, Finn perched high on the ladder like a gargoyle.

She spread her rolled blueprints on the counter. "Look."

Addison whistled. "Whoa. That's our rosette. Right there in the atrium."

Chartrand adjusted his spectacles, peering closely. "Symbols travel. Meaning does not stay politely in one place."

Marisol rubbed her forehead. "The clients noticed. They said it pulled them inward."

Finn leapt from the ladder, landing with a thud on the plans. He sat squarely on the rosette mark, tail-stub twitching, as if stamping approval.

"Traitor," Marisol muttered fondly, scratching his chin.

Addison grinned. "Maybe it's not a bad thing. If the geometry spreads, maybe it strengthens the circle here too."

Marisol frowned. "Or maybe it makes both worlds vulnerable. If he can erase here..."

The seam hummed sharply, cutting her off.

The lights flickered. The ivy wallpaper trembled. On the blueprints, the lines of the atrium warped, flattening into subtraction marks.

Marisol gasped, grabbing her compass. "He's here. In the plans."

Addison clutched the ledger. "Then redraw."

Chartrand pressed both hands to the table. "Circle him out."

Marisol set the compass, hand shaking, and traced a new arc across the vellum. The subtraction lines bent, flickered, and dissolved. Her spiral glowed faintly, ink shimmering with the shop's hum.

Finn pressed his paw on the atrium's heart. The blueprint steadied. The subtraction retreated.

The seam exhaled, the wallpaper stilled.

Marisol collapsed back, heart racing. "He's not limited to the shop anymore."

Chartrand's voice was grave. "No. He has found your other world. The price of meaning is that it spreads."

Addie whispered, "Then we'll spread faster."

Finn purred once, loud as thunder, his green eyes fierce.

That night, after customers left, Marisol unrolled her plans again. She studied the arcs, the sigils bleeding into her professional work. She thought of clients calling them "compelling," of the pale man trying to flatten them, of Finn's paw keeping the rosette steady.

Her voice shook but steadied with use. "If symbols are spreading into my life, then I'll make them ours. Not his."

She took her compass, her pencil, her ink, and added a small whisker-mark to the corner of her blueprints—a cat's sigil, Finn's mark, hidden in the detail of a column base.

"Keeper," she whispered.

Finn purred, pressed his forehead to her hand, and stayed there until the ink dried.

20 Hollows

The morning started as usual: tea steaming, rugs soft underfoot, the circle faintly glowing on the floorboards. But Addison forgot to unlock the till until a customer cleared their throat, and Mr. Chartrand returned the same book to Biography three times before realizing it was already shelved.

Marisol noticed, heart tightening. She'd felt the ache of her own sacrifices—lost tastes, missing smells—but this was different. Addison's brow furrowed when she tried to recall a boy's name in a story she loved. Chartrand stared blankly at a familiar poem as though the ink had gone faint.

The circle thrummed, steady and protective, but the toll it had taken was written on their faces.

Finn hopped onto the counter, tail-stub twitching, green eyes sharp. He nudged Addison's ledger with his head, then swiped his paw across Chartrand's notebook, scattering pages.

"Stop, Finn!" Addison protested, scooping him up. But he wriggled free, leaping onto Marisol's shoulder with surprising force. His purr was loud, insistent, vibrating into her bones like a warning bell.

"He knows," Marisol whispered.

Addison sat cross-legged on the floor by the rosette, chewing the end of her pen. "I can't remember what color the sweater was," she said, frowning. "The one I wore when I first came here. I thought it was blue, but maybe it was red? Or gray? It's just...gone."

Her voice cracked, the edges of bravado slipping. "It was supposed to be a small memory. Nothing important."

Marisol knelt beside her, resting a hand on her shoulder. "Even small things hold us together."

Addison blinked fast, eyes shining. "What if I forget bigger ones?"

Finn padded over, curling into her lap. He pressed his nose to her wrist, purr loud as if stitching something invisible back into place.

Addison stroked his fur, tears slipping free. "At least he remembers."

That afternoon, Chartrand stood at the poetry shelf, a slim volume in hand. His lips moved silently over the words. After a moment, he lowered the book, face stricken.

"I can't hear the cadence," he said softly. "I know the line, but the rhythm is gone. The heartbeat of it."

Marisol's throat ached. "That's what you gave, isn't it? A line of a poem."

"Yes." His smile was brittle. "And with it, perhaps more than I bargained."

He closed the book, setting it carefully back on the shelf. Then he leaned his forehead against the spine for a long moment, whispering something she couldn't catch.

Finn leapt up onto the shelf beside him, balancing with surprising grace. He pressed his side against Chartrand's temple, purring steadily. Chartrand chuckled softly, though his eyes were damp. "Thank you, keeper."

That night, when the shop was closed, Marisol spread her blueprints on the counter. The whisker-sigil gleamed faintly under the lamp. Her drafting world and the shop's world had merged, and now both asked for payment.

She thought of the bike ride she no longer remembered, of the stew she could no longer taste, of the smell of her pencils gone hollow. Manageable losses, until she saw Addison's confusion and Chartrand's silence.

"What if it takes too much?" she whispered. "What if it hollows us out one by one until all that's left is chalk lines and a cat?"

Finn stretched across the vellum, his small body anchoring the plans. His purr swelled, louder than her fear, vibrating into the counter itself.

Marisol closed her eyes, resting her forehead against his fur. "Then I'll give instead," she murmured. "I'll give more. So they don't have to."

Finn stilled, then headbutted her chin with surprising force, as if saying *no*. His green eyes met hers, fierce and unyielding.

"You're right," she whispered, shaken. "We'll find another way."

Before leaving, they gathered in the circle. Addison lit the stub of their communal candle. Chartrand recited a poem, faltering but steady, even if the rhythm escaped him. Marisol whispered the Keeper's word: *Hold.*

The rosette glowed faintly, not triumphant but resilient.

Finn curled at the center, eyes half-closed, purr filling the hollows Addison and Chartrand had surrendered. It wasn't enough to restore what was gone, but it was enough to remind them that not all subtraction could win.

Marisol whispered the benediction: "Goodnight, little kingdom. Hold together."

For the first time, her voice cracked, but the circle hummed back, strong as ever.

21 The Orchard Dream

Marisol fell asleep at her drafting table, her head pillowed on rolled vellum. The hum of Finn's purr lulled her, steady as surf.

She dreamed she was walking a path paved with book spines, fog curling low around her ankles. Each step whispered titles—some she remembered, some she knew had been erased. Her hand brushed the air, and a spine disappeared beneath her touch, leaving only silence.

"Careful."

The voice drifted from the mist: low, patient, carrying the weight of centuries. The Keeper.

Marisol's chest loosened. "You again."

The fog thinned, revealing the orchard: rows of apple trees in impossible bloom, white petals drifting on air that smelled of paper and earth. At the center stood the Keeper, a tall woman with hair threaded in silver, eyes the green of old ink. She leaned on a staff carved with spirals.

Finn padded at Marisol's side in the dream, tail-stub high, ears forward. His paws left prints of chalk dust in the orchard grass.

"You've learned the first cost," the Keeper said, her gaze resting on Marisol's face. "Memory, tithed willingly. Chosen. But you think that is the only price. It is not."

Marisol's throat tightened. "What else?"

The Keeper touched a branch heavy with blossoms. As her fingers brushed, several petals winked out, leaving gaps. "Memory is the smallest coin. What he subtracts, he subtracts forever. But what you bind—what you *keep*—requires more than fragments."

Marisol frowned. "We've given so much already. Addison's forgetting sweaters. Chartrand's losing rhythm. I can't ask them to give more."

The Keeper's expression softened. "Not more of memory. More of *selves*. Story. The marrow of who you are. The shop will ask it. You must decide whether to answer."

Finn hissed softly, pressing against Marisol's ankle. His eyes glowed brighter in the orchard fog, unblinking.

The Keeper drew a small circle in the dirt with her staff, spiraling outward until it became a rosette. Inside it, she placed a single apple blossom. It did not vanish. Instead, it glowed, filling the orchard with light.

"Some offerings strengthen without hollowing," she said. "An act. A story shared aloud. A truth spoken when silence tempts."

Marisol bent closer, breath catching. "You mean—there are ways to pay without losing memories?"

The Keeper's eyes gleamed. "Yes. But they demand courage of another kind. He subtracts. You must *create*."

Finn padded forward, placed his paw squarely on the blossom, and purred. The light swelled, spilling through the orchard until even the fog gleamed.

The light wavered. A dark figure moved between the trees: the pale man, his outline sharp even in a dream. He plucked blossoms as he walked, each one winking out with no sound, his pockets swelling with subtraction.

"You cannot outpace me," his voice murmured, though his lips did not move. "Even your dreams bleed into my order."

Marisol stood her ground, though her hands shook. "We're not just giving anymore. We're making."

The Keeper raised her staff, striking the ground. The rosette she'd drawn flared, repelling the man's shadow for a heartbeat. But the blossoms did not grow back.

"You cannot stop loss," the Keeper whispered. "But you can decide what remains."

Marisol gasped awake at her table. Vellum crinkled under her cheek. The lamp still glowed. Finn was curled against her arm, eyes wide open, as if he, too, had been watching the orchard. Chalk dust clung to his whiskers.

She sat up, dizzy. On the blueprint before her, a blossom shape had been sketched in faint graphite, though she had not drawn it.

"Not memory," she whispered. "But story. Truth."

Finn sneezed, scattering dust, then placed one paw deliberately on the blossom mark. His purr filled the room, loud and certain.

Marisol pressed her hand beside his. "Then we'll create. Whatever it takes."

22 Making to Keep

The next morning, Marisol unlocked Ink & Ivy with the Keeper's words echoing: *You must create.* The rosette glowed faintly under the rugs, the chalk spirals steady but subdued, as though waiting.

Addison burst in with her sketchpad tucked under her arm. "I've been thinking," she said breathlessly. "What if we give it drawings instead of memories?"

Mr. Chartrand followed, carrying a sheaf of poems written in his neat hand. "Or verses," he added. "Words made new."

Finn trotted between them, tail-stub upright like a banner. He leapt to the counter and pawed at Marisol's notebook, urging.

Marisol smiled despite her fatigue. "Then today we test. Not what we've lost. What we make."

Addison sat cross-legged on the floor inside the rosette. She flipped open her sketchpad and began drawing with quick, bold strokes: Finn, perched imperiously atop the seam, tail flicking, eyes glowing.

As her pencil moved, the chalk spirals pulsed brighter. The seam hummed, not nervously but curiously. The shelves leaned forward, listening.

She tore out the page and laid it in the circle. The drawing shimmered, then settled, as though absorbed into the pattern. A spine that had been dulled in Folklore regained its color.

Addison gasped. "It worked. It *worked!*"

Finn strutted over, sat squarely on his own likeness, and began washing his paw with smug thoroughness.

Chartrand cleared his throat, adjusting his spectacles. He unfolded a page and began to read, voice low but resonant:

"*The circle widens, not to exclude, but to gather.*
The chalk is dust, yet dust is memory. What we trace, we keep. What we speak, we mend."

As he spoke, the words drifted into the rosette, visible like faint smoke. The chalk lines glowed warmer, golden rather than white. In Mythology, a gap closed halfway, the missing outline sharpening.

Chartrand lowered the page, cheeks flushed. "Not Shakespeare," he said softly, "but it seems to please the shop."

Finn headbutted his shin, purr rising in clear agreement.

Marisol hesitated, heart pounding. Drawing and poetry had worked. What could she give?

She rolled a scrap of vellum across the counter, set her compass, and drew a perfect circle. Then another, shifted by a degree, until a rosette bloomed. She pressed it into the rosette on the floor, whispering:

"This is not for clients. Not for Isley. Not for blueprints. It's for you."

The vellum shimmered, sank into the chalk as if the floor itself swallowed it whole. The seam hummed a deeper note, steady and strong. One of the ledger's blank outlines filled in fully, a book title reappearing in neat script: *Songs of the Cedar Wind.*

Marisol's eyes burned. She remembered reading it once at sixteen, pages smelling of dust and pine. She hadn't realized it had vanished until it returned.

Addie clapped. "You gave it back!"

Chartrand smiled faintly. "Creation restores what subtraction would erase."

Finn yowled once, sharp and triumphant, the sound ringing through the shop like a bell.

That afternoon, customers wandered in unaware yet drawn to the energy. A teenager sat in the circle, doodling dragons in the corner of her notebook. The chalk pulsed faintly, approving.

An elderly man read aloud a limerick to his granddaughter, both laughing. The shelves shivered, pleased.

A woman hummed softly as she browsed. The seam steadied.

Marisol caught Chartrand's eye across the room. "They don't even know," she whispered. "But every act of making feeds it."

Chartrand nodded gravely. "He subtracts. We multiply."

When the last customer left, they gathered again in the circle. Addison spread her drawings, Chartrand laid down his poems, and Marisol placed her rosette sketch. The floor hummed, symbols glowing softly.

Marisol whispered: "Goodnight, little kingdom. Hold together."

Addison added: "And grow."

Chartrand placed his palm on the seam. "And remember."

Finn curled at the heart of the circle, his purr filling the shop until even the ivy wallpaper seemed to breathe with it.

Outside, winter pressed hard against the glass, efficient and subtractive. Inside, creation glowed stubborn and warm.

23 Mockery

The next morning, Ink & Ivy smelled faintly of paper and cinnamon—comforting as always. Addison arrived with a new drawing, a fox curled around a book. She laid it proudly inside the rosette.

For a moment, the chalk pulsed warm. Then the drawing shifted. The fox's eyes narrowed, its grin sharpening until the page looked like it was sneering. The book in its paws dissolved into a blank rectangle.

Addison gasped, snatching the page back. "That's not what I drew."

Mr. Chartrand bent close, frowning. "He's learned to twist our gifts."

Finn stalked forward, tail bristling. He leapt onto the page, shredding it with a flurry of claws until the warped fox was nothing but paper tatters. He sat on the scraps, glaring at the seam, a growl rattling low in his chest.

The seam hummed faintly, mocking.

That afternoon, Chartrand stood in the circle with a new verse he had written in the early hours:

"Even the smallest line resists the void. Even the faintest hum holds back silence."

The words left his lips strong. But as they drifted into the rosette, they bent. The hum twisted thin, the verse reshaped into:

"Even the strongest line dissolves. Even the deepest hum fades."

Chartrand's face paled. "That's not mine."

The shelves shivered uneasily, spines trembling.

Marisol grabbed his hand, gripping tight. "It isn't you. It's him."

Finn yowled, springing to Chartrand's feet. He pressed his body against the old man's shin, purr loud, steady, drowning out the warped echo. Slowly, the shelves calmed.

Chartrand bent, stroking Finn's head, tears bright in his eyes. "Thank you, keeper."

Marisol unrolled a sheet of vellum across the counter that evening. She drew a rosette with her compass, steady hand tracing arcs with care. For a heartbeat, the chalk circle glowed brighter.

Then the vellum warped. The arcs bent into grids, angles crisp, circles erased. Where her rosette had been, a perfect square remained.

Her chest constricted. "He's mocking me. Turning creation into subtraction."

Addison grabbed the vellum. "We can burn it!"

But Finn leapt first, sprawling across the warped square. His claws dug, shredding the lines into nonsense. He rolled onto his back, scattering chalk dust with his stub-tail, reclaiming the page as play.

The square dissolved. The chalk circle steadied again.

Marisol dropped to her knees, burying her face in Finn's fur. "You saved it."

He purred, triumphant, as though to say: *Not on my watch.*

That night, a boy sat in the rosette, doodling a dragon. When he finished, he frowned. "Why does it look...wrong?"

The dragon's eyes were blank, wings crooked, mouth frozen open in a scream.

His mother pulled him back quickly. "Let's draw at home." She crumpled the page, but the boy's hands shook.

Another customer hummed a tune absentmindedly. The notes bent flat, spiraling into silence before she stopped, startled.

Marisol's blood chilled. The pale man wasn't only twisting their offerings. He was corrupting customers' unknowing gifts, too.

She pressed both palms to the circle. "*Hold,*" she whispered. The chalk pulsed faintly, fighting, but it felt weaker than before.

Exhausted, they gathered at closing. The warped fox, the twisted poem, the square rosette, the boy's dragon—all evidence of the pale man's intrusion.

"He's not subtracting," Addison whispered. "He's mocking. Turning everything upside down."

Chartrand's voice trembled. "Which is worse. Subtraction, we can track. But mockery poisons what we love."

Marisol looked at them both, then at Finn curled in the circle. His green eyes glowed steadily.

"Then we offer something he can't twist," she said. "Not drawings. Not poems. Not vellum. Something alive. A truth."

She drew a breath, then spoke into the circle: "I'm afraid every day. Afraid I'll fail you. Afraid he'll win. But I'm still here."

The chalk flared. The seam hummed louder, resonant. A book that had been trembling in Mythology stilled, its spine brightening.

Addison blinked. "It worked. Because it was...real."

Chartrand nodded slowly. "Truth resists mockery."

Finn purred, long and low, curling tighter around the circle's center. His purr was its own truth: stubborn, alive, unaltered.

They locked the doors late. Marisol whispered her benediction, voice rough: "Goodnight, little kingdom. Hold together."

Addison added: "Don't let him twist us."

Chartrand placed his palm on the seam. "May what we make remain true."

Finn leapt to Marisol's shoulder as they turned out the lamps. He pressed his head against her jaw, purr steady, his body warm as fire.

Outside, the frost deepened. Inside, the circle glowed faintly—not unlocked, but still theirs.

And in the silence between shelves, the pale man's laugh lingered, thin as paper torn.

24 Fracture

The next evening, the hum beneath the floorboards carried a new discord: not steady, not soft, but sharp, like glass scored by a knife.

Marisol froze mid-shelving, a paperback in her hand. She knelt, lifting the rug from the center aisle. The rosette lay exposed—chalk faint, vellum edges curling, ink marks dimmed. But worse: a hairline crack ran through it, splitting Finn's whisker-sigil in two.

Her chest tightened. "No. No, no, no."

Addison gasped. "It's breaking."

Chartrand's hand trembled as he adjusted his spectacles. "It's under too much strain. Subtraction has pressed too long. The circle is...failing."

Finn darted to the crack, pressing his paw to it, meowing sharply and loudly. The seam groaned, the shelves rattled. A book fell from History, its spine blurred as though half-erased.

Marisol's pulse raced. "We can't patch it with chalk anymore. It needs something more."

Wordless unease spread to the patrons. A teenager frowned at the cookbook in her hand. "Why are the pages blank?"

A man at the counter blinked rapidly, whispering, "I don't remember what I came for."

The lights flickered overhead. The ivy wallpaper peeled slightly at the corners, curling away as though retreating.

Marisol leapt onto the counter, heart hammering. "Read! All of you—anything, aloud!"

The room filled with shaky voices: recipes, poems, chapter titles. But their words wavered, thinning, slipping like water through cupped hands.

Addison clutched the ledger. "It's not enough. It's not holding."

Finn yowled again, voice slicing the air. His fur bristled, tail stiff, eyes blazing green. He planted himself squarely on the crack, but even his weight couldn't hold it closed.

The glass of the front windows frosted over suddenly, opaque as paper painted white. A whisper slithered through the shop, not loud but everywhere at once:

"Circles always close. And closing means ending."

Marisol shook her head violently. "No."

The chalk lines bent under unseen pressure, spirals straightening into angles, Chartrand's rune warping into subtraction marks. Addison's sketches curled, their foxes and dragons grinning too wide.

Marisol grabbed her compass, her pencil, and her ink and dropped to her knees. Her voice cracked: "We'll redraw. We'll hold."

Her hand shook too badly to guide the compass. The pencil snapped under the strain.

Marisol froze, staring at the fracture splitting Finn's sigil. Her fear swelled, bitter and choking. *I'm afraid every day.* She had said it once. The Keeper's words echoed: *You must create. You must decide what remains.*

Her boldest choice crystallized in the silence: not chalk, not vellum, not words borrowed from books, but her.

She pressed her palm directly to the crack. "Take me," she whispered. "Not my memories. My fear. My silence. Take what weakens me, and I'll give it willingly."

The circle flared, light spilling up her arm, burning but not painful. The fracture glowed, then sealed with a sound like a bell rung clear.

Books settled. Shelves stilled. Customers blinked, confusion clearing from their faces.

Finn leapt onto her shoulder, claws digging gently into her sweater, his purr vibrating like thunder.

Addison gasped. "Marisol—you—what did you do?"

Marisol's chest heaved. Her voice shook, but steadied as she said it aloud: "I gave him my fear."

The pale man's whisper rose again, colder this time: *"Fear feeds me more than memory."*

But the circle glowed brighter, its chalk lines re-drawn in light, not dust. The whisker-sigil pulsed strongest of all, whole again.

Marisol stood shakily. "Maybe. But I chose it. You can't twist what I give freely."

A rumble passed through the shop, like distant thunder. The frosted windows cracked, splintered, then cleared, revealing the night outside dark but honest. The pale man was gone.

Chartrand exhaled shakily. "You've done what none of us dared. Not a tithe. A surrender."

Addison reached for Marisol's hand. "And you're still you."

Marisol smiled faintly, exhausted but steady. "I'm still here. And so is the shop."

Finn purred, sprawling across both her shoulders now as though he had carried her through. His warmth filled the hollow fear that had been left behind.

That night, after customers departed, they sat cross-legged around the restored rosette. Chartrand read softly, Addison sketched again—this time the fox curled peacefully, not twisted. Marisol leaned into Finn's steady warmth, letting the hum of the circle wrap around her.

Her benediction was quieter than usual, but stronger for it: "Goodnight, little kingdom. Hold together."

The rosette glowed, uncracked, steady.

For the first time, Marisol didn't whisper the words from fear. She whispered them as a promise.

25 The Intrusion

It was a Wednesday evening, the kind of night when winter pressed close and the shop glowed golden against the dark. Marisol had just poured tea, Addison had curled in a corner with her sketchpad, Chartrand was shelving Poetry, and Finn was asleep on the counter, stub-tail flicking in a dream.

Then the bell above the front door did not ring. The door swung wide without sound. Cold spilled in, white and empty.

And the pale man stepped inside.

He wore no coat despite the snow. His pale eyes roved the shelves with clinical precision. When he closed the door behind him, silence thickened like frost. Even Finn's purr cut off mid-breath.

"Your circle holds," the pale man said, voice calm, every syllable exact. "But circles cannot bar the one who is subtraction itself."

He walked slowly down Fiction, fingertip trailing spines. Where he touched, titles blurred. A novel lost its cover art, a spine turned gray. He moved as though inspecting inventory he already owned.

Customers froze mid-browse. A woman at the till whispered, "Who is that?" Her voice came out thin, almost erased.

Marisol stepped into the aisle, heart hammering. "Stop."

The pale man tilted his head. "I am inevitable. You keep what should not be kept. You clutter order with story. You have given me your fear, and I am stronger for it."

Finn leapt from the counter to the floor, hackles raised, hiss splitting the silence like torn paper. He darted in front of Marisol, planting himself between her and the pale man.

The rosette pulsed from beneath the rug, faint light seeping upward. Chalk lines brightened, spirals trembling as though ready to spin. The pale man paused, lips tightening.

"This geometry is stubborn," he said softly. "It resists."

Marisol lifted the rug in one swift motion, exposing the glowing rosette. "Because it isn't geometry. It's a story."

Addison and Chartrand rushed to her side. Addison dropped her sketchpad into the circle—today's drawing of Finn sitting atop a stack of books. Chartrand opened his notebook and read aloud, his voice shaking but clear:

"*What we trace, we keep. What we speak, we mend.*"

The rosette flared brighter.

The pale man's face remained impassive, but his eyes narrowed slightly. "Creation falters. It bends. And I bend it further."

He raised his hand. The fox Addison had drawn days before reappeared on the wall, sneering, eyes empty. Chartrand's verse echoed back warped: *Even the deepest hum fades.*

The rosette flickered, caught between light and shadow. Customers stumbled, blinking, their books blurring in their hands.

Marisol clenched her fists. "Truth resists mockery."

Her voice shook, but she stepped into the circle and shouted: "I was afraid of failing. But I am not afraid of *you.*"

The rosette surged, spirals burning bright. Books stilled. Shelves straightened.

Finn leapt into the circle, yowling. His paw landed square on his whisker-sigil. The sound was so loud it rattled the glass.

The pale man flinched. For the first time, his perfect face twisted with something almost human, distaste.

The ivy wallpaper rustled as though a breeze passed through. A faint voice threaded the air, the Keeper's echo: You are not alone.

The pale man's pale eyes darted toward the sound. His outline flickered, the edges of his form blurring.

"You weaken me only for now," he said coldly. "You cannot keep forever. Subtraction waits."

He stepped back toward the door. Each stride dimmed the lights, each breath frosted the glass. But when he reached the threshold, the bell above the door rang. Clear. Bright. Defiant.

His figure dissolved into the night.

The shop exhaled. Customers blinked, murmuring, unaware of how close they had been to vanishing. One woman shook her head. "Strange draft," she muttered. She bought her book and left.

Chartrand slumped into a chair, breath ragged. Addison wiped her eyes.

Marisol dropped to her knees in the circle, hands trembling. "He was *here*."

Finn climbed onto her lap, pressing his whole body against her. His purr thundered, filling the hollows subtraction had left.

"We held," Addison whispered. "We actually held."

Chartrand's voice shook. "But he'll come again. Directly. More forcefully."

Marisol looked at the rosette, glowing faintly but steadily. She stroked Finn's fur, her hand calming with each pass.

"Then so will we," she said. "We'll be ready."

They closed late, locking the door twice over. Together they stood at the circle. Addison laid her fox drawing down again, this time softened into kindness. Chartrand placed his notebook beside it. Marisol pressed her compass to the floor.

"Goodnight, little kingdom," she whispered. "Hold together."

Finn purred, sprawling across all three offerings as though claiming them. His green eyes met hers, fierce and steady.

For the first time, Marisol believed the pale man had reason to fear them.

26 The Last Subtraction

Ink & Ivy felt wrong the moment Marisol unlocked the door. The air was heavy, not with dust or winter chill, but with silence pressed too close, like an eraser poised above paper.

The chalk circle was already glowing faintly, as if bracing itself. The whisker-sigil pulsed like a heartbeat.

Addison arrived pale, sketchpad clutched tight. "I dreamed he walked the orchard again. Only this time, he touched every blossom."

Chartrand followed with weary eyes. "I dreamed he touched every book."

Finn padded in after them, tail high, but his ears flattened. He darted straight into the circle and sat, growling low, refusing to leave.

Marisol closed the door, her voice steady though her stomach turned: "It's today."

It started with the shelves. One by one, spines blurred, titles dissolving into faint gray. Cookbooks became blank paper. Mystery novels lost their twists. A child's picture book in a girl's hands faded as she turned the page. She gasped and dropped it, whispering, "It's gone."

Then the ivy wallpaper withered, leaves curling black. The seam groaned low, rattling the floorboards.

The front door burst open without a sound. Snow swirled in, white and endless. The pale man stepped across the threshold. This time, he did not speak. He simply raised both hands.

Every book in the shop shuddered.

Marisol stepped into the rosette, voice breaking: "*Hold!*"

The circle flared, spirals glowing bright. Addison dropped to her knees, sketching fast: Finn on the counter, Finn at the window, Finn chasing dust motes. Each drawing shimmered as it touched the circle, then warped, but she shouted truth over them: "He *is* joy. He *is* ours."

Chartrand read aloud, voice ragged but resolute:

"*Not silence but sound, not ending but telling. We mend by making, we keep by choosing.*"

The warped echoes tried to twist his words, but Finn leapt, yowling, his cry breaking the echo apart like glass.

The Keeper's voice thrummed faintly from the ivy walls: *What you keep, you must name.*

The pale man's pale eyes locked on Marisol. He stepped into the circle itself. The chalk cracked beneath his shoes. Spirals dimmed.

Marisol's chest seized with terror. *Fear feeds me,* he had once said. And yet—she had given her fear already. What else could he claim?

Then it struck her: the Keeper's warning. Not just memory. Not just fear. *Story.*

She lifted her chin. "I name what we keep."

She pressed her hand to the floor, voice steady despite trembling:

- "Addison keeps her laughter, even when it cracks.
- Chartrand keeps his rhythm, even when it falters.
- I keep this shop, even when the shelves tremble.
- And Finn—" she broke off, tears thick—"Finn keeps *all of us.*"

The circle blazed, brighter than lamps, brighter than snow light. The pale man staggered, his form flickering, edges blurring.

Finn sprang to the crack in the rosette and stood tall. His small body glowed with the whisker-sigil, light spilling from his fur. He opened his mouth and yowled—not a sound of fear, but of claim.

Every book answered. Spines gleamed, titles sharpened, pages fluttered. Customers gasped as their forgotten words returned. The shelves leaned inward, protecting.

The pale man snarled, a sound like paper ripping. He reached for Finn.

But the cat leapt higher, straight into Marisol's arms, pressing his paw to her chest. The sigil's light spread across her, then into Addison, then into Chartrand. The three of them glowed together, one circle made flesh.

"*We keep,*" they shouted as one.

The pale man's form buckled, folding inward as though it was erased stroke by stroke. His pale eyes dimmed. His lips moved once: *"Circles close."*

Marisol whispered back, fierce and steady: "Not this one."

With a final flare, the circle sealed. The pale man dissolved into snow, then into nothing.

Silence, fell—true silence, not subtractive, but clean. The shop hummed low, steady, alive.

Customers blinked, confused but unharmed. Books rested on shelves whole. The ivy wallpaper greened again. The ledger was filled with titles where gaps had been.

Chartrand sank into a chair, tears streaming silently. Addison clutched her sketchpad to her chest, laughing and sobbing in the same breath.

Marisol stood trembling in the circle, Finn pressed to her heart, his purr loud and steady.

She whispered, not in fear but in promise: "Goodnight, little kingdom. Hold together."

The shop hummed back, stronger than ever, as though answering: *We will.*

The customers drifted out one by one, murmuring thanks, none aware of how close they had come to erasure. Marisol locked the door behind them, her hand lingering on the key. The bell above it chimed softly, sweet and ordinary.

Inside, Ink & Ivy looked almost unchanged: rugs rumpled, chalk dust scattered, a faint glow still pulsing beneath the rosette. Yet to Marisol every detail felt sharper, brighter, more alive. The spines gleamed, the ivy wallpaper rustled faintly as though pleased, and the air smelled of paper and tea instead of subtraction.

Addison stretched out across the counter, her sketchpad open. She began doodling absentmindedly—cats chasing moths, stacks of books that spiraled upward. The lines stayed true. No warping.

Chartrand sat in the poetry section, reading aloud softly to himself, his voice regaining its rhythm. His smile was tired but real.

Finn prowled the aisles like a small, victorious sentinel, stopping often to butt his head against the shelves, as though reassuring them one by one.

Marisol brewed a pot of chamomile and brought three mugs to the circle. They sat cross-legged in its glow, the rugs bunched beneath them.

"To keeping," Addison said, lifting her mug.

"To choosing," Chartrand added, voice quiet but steady.

Marisol stroked Finn, who had sprawled across her lap, purr deep and triumphant. She lifted her mug last. "To stories."

They drank in silence, the kind of silence that was full rather than empty.

When the mugs were empty and the lamps dim, Marisol whispered the benediction. Her voice no longer trembled. "Goodnight, little kingdom. Hold together."

Addison added softly: "Grow strong."

Chartrand's voice was reverent: "Remember us."

Finn gave a single sharp meow, tail flicking, as if sealing the promise.

The circle glowed faintly under the rugs, no longer strained, simply steady. Outside, snow fell in soft, ordinary flakes that melted on the glass.

Marisol leaned back, letting her head rest against the counter, Finn warm against her. For the first time in weeks, she let her eyes close without dread. The shop hummed around them like a lullaby.
And in that hum was a truth she finally believed: the kingdom would hold.

Epilogue

Morning light slanted across Marisol's drafting desk, pooling on stacks of vellum. The firm had finally given her the mezzanine project outright, and she bent over it now, pencil poised, compass steady.

Her hand moved easily, drawing arcs that curved toward each other, rosettes forming without strain. No one blinked twice anymore. Isley, grudging at first, had begun to call them "signature details," and clients leaned in with admiration rather than suspicion.

"Feels...alive," one had murmured last week, running a finger along her plans.

She smiled at the memory as she adjusted the compass. Arcs intersected into petals, opening space rather than boxing it. She knew the Keeper's words still lingered in her work, but now she wasn't afraid of it. Geometry and story could live together.

A thump interrupted her thoughts. She turned. Finn sprawled across the corner of her drafting table, tail-stub twitching dangerously close to her ink jar.

"Don't you dare," she warned.

He tipped the jar over with one paw. Ink spread like a comet across the margin of her vellum.

Marisol laughed despite herself. "Fine. A little of you in every plan."

After office hours, she walked the few blocks to Ink & Ivy, scarf wound tight against the cold. The windows glowed golden against the dark, ivy wallpaper catching the lamplight. Inside, the bell chimed as she pushed the door open.

Addison was behind the counter, humming as she finished a sketch of a fox that actually looked mischievous instead of sinister. Chartrand sat in the poetry section, reading softly to a cluster of regulars who had begun to treat Thursday nights as a standing appointment.

Finn barreled toward her, tail high, leaping onto her shoulder as though she were late. His purr vibrated against her ear.

"Miss me that much?" she whispered, stroking his fur.

The shop hummed in greeting, spirals faintly glowing beneath the rugs. Customers browsed untroubled, and every spine on the shelves gleamed intact. The ledger sat open on the counter, no gaps waiting to be filled.

Marisol breathed deep. Home, in both senses of the word.

Finn made himself the evening's

entertainment. He batted pens off the counter with surgical precision, chased a rogue bookmark under Biography, and sprawled across the poetry circle during Chartrand's reading until two lines had to be repeated over his purring.

When Addison laughed too hard, he leapt into her lap, demanding tribute scratches. When a customer sneezed, he darted to the History section as though hunting the culprit.

Marisol watched it all with amused exasperation. "You know you're not subtle," she told him when he returned to her shoulder.

He butted her chin hard enough to sting, eyes gleaming. Subtlety, clearly, was not the point.

Later, when the last customer left, Finn flopped across the ledger, rolling until his whisker-sigil smudged faintly into the page. The chalk lines beneath the rug pulsed in response, amused.

Marisol shook her head. "Keeper of chaos."

But her voice was warm, full of gratitude.

Closing time was gentler now. Addison tidied her sketches into a folder, Chartrand placed his book reverently back on the shelf, and Marisol brewed chamomile in the small kettle behind the counter. They carried their mugs to the rosette, sitting cross-legged as always.

"To story," Addison said, raising her mug.

"To rhythm," Chartrand added.

"To keeping," Marisol finished.

Finn purred loudly enough to drown them all out, sprawled across her lap as though he had been the point all along.

When the lamps dimmed and the door was locked, Marisol whispered her benediction with calm certainty: "Goodnight, little kingdom. Hold together."

The shelves hummed back, ivy leaves rustling faintly. Outside, snow fell in soft, ordinary flakes, no longer subtractive but simply winter.

Marisol stroked Finn's fur, listening to the steady thrum of his purr. Her life balanced now between blueprints and books, arcs and stories, the practical and the impossible.

The little kingdom had held. And so had she.

Some days I am drafting mezzanines, measured in steel and concrete. Other days, I am tending shelves, measured in ink and memory. Both lives hum beneath my hands now, and I no longer try to separate them. The circle is here, in vellum arcs and chalk spirals, in whispered benedictions and the steady weight of Finn curled across my lap. We've learned that what we keep is not only books, but ourselves — laughter, rhythm, courage, and the stubborn will to mend what subtraction would erase. Tonight, the shop is quiet, the tea is warm, the shelves breathe softly in their sleep. Finn purrs. And I believe, for the first time without fear, that the little kingdom will hold.

— Marisol Callan

About the Author

Angela Grey is an Indigenous novelist, poet, and painter whose work explores the intersections of memory, identity, and healing. She, formerly an architectural drafter, studied creative writing, as well as spirituality and healing, at the University of Minnesota, where she deepened her commitment to storytelling as both an art and a form of medicine. Alongside her writing, Angela finds balance in yoga and Mindfulness-Based Stress Reduction (MBSR), which shapes the reflective quality of her work. She lives in Eden Prairie, Minnesota, with her husband, one spirited pup, and four cats. When she's not writing, she enjoys camping, budget travel to places like Maine, Oregon, and the coastal Carolinas, and gathering with family around a BBQ grill.

Website: ShadyOakPress.com
Website: angelagrey.com
Tiktok: @authorAngelaGrey
Instagram: angelaellengrey
Facebook: angelaellengrey
Twitter: @AngelaEllenGrey

9 781961 841529